Origin of the Lights and Other Stories

A Furry Short Story Collection

Ian Madison Keller

Rainbow Dog

Rainbow Dog Books

Contents

1. Milk and Brass   1

2. The Monster in the Mist   19

3. Northern Delights   43

4. Suddenly, Chihuahua   81

5. The Church Mouse   103

6. Bucking the Trend   127

7. The Pine Lesson   143

8. The White Deer   167

9. Fate's answer   193

10. Cyrano's Companion   197

11. The Fish and the Candles   203

12. Origin of the Lights   205

Also By Ian Madison Keller   210

About the Author   212

Milk and Brass

This story was originally published in *Purrfect Tails* edited by Tarl Hoch and released by Armoured Fox Press in April 2018.

A commotion farther down the alley in which Carla had chosen to bed down that night woke her. She peered out from the cardboard box she'd curled up in, cat ears swiveling and tail twitching with curiosity.

Blue uniformed Bobbies were moving down the line of sleeping vagrants, waking them with vicious kicks or strikes with their billy clubs. Growls, shrieks, and grumbles were left behind in their wake as the various human-animal hybrids were rousted and hauled away towards the Paddy wagon parked blocking the alley's end.

"You, cat-hybrid." An approaching Bobby had noticed her gleaming eyes and pointed to her with the end of his club. "Up and at-em. We've got a place in the work-house all picked out for you."

The work-house. She'd only just barely escaped alive from her last imprisonment there. Filthy beds, grueling hours, not enough food. No, she wouldn't go back.

Carla bolted from her cardboard box, abandoning her few meager possessions. The other end of the alley ended in a tall wooden fence. Carla's bare feet pounded down the cobblestones, easily out pacing the Bobby behind her. She jumped as she approached the fence, vaulting over it with one smooth leap.

Before the Bobby crashed into the wood she was already gone, dashing down the street. However, the young Bobby's cries alerted the rest to her flight. By the time she rounded the corner, two more were in pursuit, whistles blowing.

Carla ducked and wove through the dark streets of London, but the Bobbies were tenacious. Before she knew it, they'd chased her away from the docks and into a nicer part of town. An area she didn't know.

Trees rustled somewhere ahead, the perfect place to lose her pursuers. Unfortunately, there was a wall between her and the trees. Carla rushed at it and jumped, hooking her fingers over the top. She pulled herself up and rolled over, dropping into a large private garden. Carla darted through the trees and bushes to climb up a random tree with a thick trunk. The trunk split about halfway up, leaving a perfect hollow for her to curl up in that didn't leave her visible from the ground.

There was a commotion at the end of the garden as the men reached the wall. Rather than climbing up over after her, they circled in, kicking open a gate somewhere out of sight.

"Here, kitty-kitty," they called, leaves crunched between each step. They split up, moving about the garden.

"Hey, you!" A female voice yelled. "This is a private garden. Get out!"

"We lost our kitty, and she hopped over your fence there. Soon as we find her we'll get out."

"Leave now!"

Footsteps and a short scuffle ensued. A wooden gate banged shut, but the men continued to move about on the other sides of the wall. Carla pulled herself into a tighter ball and settled in to wait.

Chirping birds and the clatter of plates woke Carla the next morning. The tantalizing aroma of toast and fried eggs wafted to her on the breeze. Carla sniffed and crawled out on a big branch, trying to glimpse the feast. Instead, she saw a young English Lady, around her age, wearing a white and yellow lacy morning dress and a hat. She sat on a patio overlooking the garden eating her breakfast.

An older woman wearing a servant's gown came outside with a steaming platter of pastries and set it next to the young Lady.

"Anything else, Miss Hanson?"

"No, thank you," the girl replied.

The maid bustled out, leaving the Lady alone on the porch. So much food, too much for one person. Perhaps she would share? Carla licked her lips and crept closer, peering out through the leaves. There was a crack and her branch dipped. Carla froze, but it was too late. The branch cracked again and pitched forward, sending Carla tumbling head over tail out of the tree with a yowl.

"Kitty?" The Lady stood, eyes searching the garden. "Are you alright kitty?"

Carla sat up, no worse for wear. She'd got her hands up in time to save her face, cat-like reflexes had their benefits.

"Here, kitty-kitty. I have eggs." The Lady scooped eggs onto a dish and carried down the steps. She set it on the path in the garden, then stood on tiptoes to look in Carla's direction. "Kitty, are you hungry?"

The food looked so good, and the Lady didn't look dangerous. Carla's tail twitched. A few bites couldn't hurt. After the English Lady went back up to the patio, Carla crept forward, keeping herself low to the ground. Her pointed cat-ears swiveled, alert for any noise.

To get to the plate she'd have to cross a large expanse of cut grass with no cover. If she was quick, she might grab the plate and dive back into the safety of the trees. Carla moved up into a sprinters crouch, digging in her toes. Now! She burst from cover, pumping her arms, eyes fixated on the eggs. The English Lady looked up from her scones, eyes widening as Carla flashed past the patio, scooping up the plate without even slowing down.

Back in the safety of the bushes, Carla ducked behind the trunk of a tree and stuffed eggs in her mouth with one hand, scalding her fingers and burning the roof of her mouth. When the plate was empty Carla licked it of every drop of grease.

"Are you hurt?" The English Lady's voice came from the side.

Carla froze, ears flattening to the top of her head and tail thrashing. The Lady stood just a few feet away, bright gown and slippers looking incongruous among the dirt and leaves. What Carla's thought was lace

4

turned out to be white feathers growing out of her arms.

"You are cut," the Lady pointed at a trail of blood on Carla's bare arm. "I can clean that for you if you'd like. And if you are still hungry, there is plenty. More than enough to share."

Carla searched the Lady's face for any trace of deceit, noting the fine white down. Her expression was open and friendly, eager to help. "I am still hungry, thank you."

"I'm Nellie." The Lady, Nellie, reached out a white gloved hand to Carla.

"Pleased to meet you, Nellie. I'm Carla." Carla curtsied in her torn and stained skirts. After she stood again, she took Nellie's hand. The gloves turned out not to be gloves at all, but soft white feathers that covered the backs of her hands.

Nellie smiled and led Carla to the porch. "You must be the kitty those men were looking for last night."

"Yes, but please don't tell anyone I am here. I..." Carla shuddered. "I can't go back to the workhouse."

Nellie squeezed her hand as Carla sat. "Have tea and scones and tell me your story. Perhaps I can help."

Carla told Nellie her tale in between bites of the delicious food. About growing up as a cat-hybrid on the streets of London, fighting for scraps. She couldn't remember what had happened to her parents, just that she'd always been alone. The first time the Bobbies found her, sent her to the workhouse, she'd been so excited. It sounded wonderful. Fed every day, a bed to sleep on. But the reality had left her starving, exhausted, unable to leave.

When she finished, Nellie frowned, eyes glistening with tears. "That's awful, Carla. I wish there was something I could do to help."

"You've done so already, Nellie." Carla licked butter from her fingers, blessedly full for the first time since she couldn't remember when. Her black tail curled in her lap and her ears perked forward.

"Perhaps I can do more. I imagine those men will be back around, hunting for you." Nellie drummed her downy fingers on the table. "I want to help you."

"Why do you want to help me?" Carla tensed, ready to bolt. "We've only just met."

"I may not be able to escape my fate, but I want to help you escape yours." The back door rattled, cutting Nellie short. "Quick, you can't be seen. Climb up to my room and wait there for me." Nellie pointed to a window on the second story.

Carla nodded, wondering what horrible fate a rich Lady like Nellie could be facing. Nellie had been sincere and Carla trusted her. The climb up was an easy one; an ivy-covered lattice covered the back wall of the house and Carla scaled it and was inside the open window before the door below finished opening.

"Dearie me, Miss Hanson. Thought I heard voices out here."

"Just talking to myself, Mrs. Norwood." There was a rustle of skirts. "I'm going to my room to change before Mr. Rogerson's visit."

"Good idea, Miss." Dishes clanked and the back door opened and closed again.

Carla crawled across the carpet and wriggled under the massive four-poster bed, heart pounding. Who was Mr. Rogerson?

Underneath the bed was dusty and Carla had to fight back a sneeze as the door opened.

"Carla?" Nellie whispered.

"Who's Mr. Rogerson?" Carla asked, not moving from her safe spot pressed up against the wall, tail curled around her side.

Nellie sighed, skirts rustling. The bed above Carla creaked as she sat. "The fate I can't escape. He is my father's friend, and my father offered him my hand in marriage." Nellie sniffled.

Carla wriggled out from under the bed. Tears sparkled in Nellie's eyes and she twisted a handkerchief in her hands, but her face was dry. Carla took her hand anyway. Nellie's feathers tickled her palms. "You don't love him?"

"I don't even like him!" Now the tears fell. Carla gently took the cloth and dabbed at her face as Nellie talked. "He's as old as my father, a widow. His wife died last year of consumption. He has three children, the oldest is less than a year younger than me."

"I'm sorry."

Nellie took the cloth from her and let out a smile between her tears. "No, I am. I shouldn't have burdened you with that. Let's get you a clean dress."

Nellie stood and bustled away to her wardrobe where she sorted through dresses. "Good thing you're about the same size as me, but your coloring is so much darker than mine. All my dresses are pastel." Nellie's eyes flicked to Carla's ears and tail. "The skirt will hide your tail, but the ears..." she made a humming sound and went back to sorting.

"I'm a black cat-hybrid," Carla replied as Nellie held dresses up to her. "Um, if I can ask, what are you?"

"Swan." Nellie made a face at her over the dresses. "Horrible birds if you ask me. Their call sounds like someone strangled a goose, plus they're mean. I wish my father had picked a songbird, like a robin or something. At least then I'd be able to carry a tune."

"I think the white feathers are pretty."

"Pretty, and not much else." Nellie came over with a blue night dress. "Here, I think this should fit you right enough."

Carla carefully took the blue robe and laid it out on the bed. Her skin was filthy from being on the run and she didn't want to get it dirty. Carla stripped out of her stained skirts. "Perhaps a bath first?"

Nellie blushed a pretty shade of red under her down and stared at the floor. "Um, water basin and washcloth are right there." She pointed without looking up.

The water was cool, but the washcloth was soft and fluffy. If she could purr, she would have. Sadly, her maker had gone with more practical traits like reflexes, night vision, cat-hearing, and a tail to help her balance. As Carla scrubbed grime off her skin, she watched Nellie from under half-closed eyes. Nellie was embarrassed at Carla's nudity, yet drawn to it. She kept glancing over at Carla when she thought she wasn't looking.

Carla had to admit a certain fascination herself. Nellie's shiny black hair and white feathers were a striking combination. Carla wanted to run her fingers through those silky tresses and pet her soft feathers. The thought gave her a tight sensation in her stomach. She'd laid with men in the past, but it had never been like this with them. This was something new, and exciting, and Carla wanted to savor the moment. Carla washed herself slowly, paying particular attention to her breasts and ass. When cleaning her arms, Carla extended her limbs up and out, finding excuses to flaunt her wide hips, rounded bottom, and black-furred tail in Nellie's direction. Nellie flushed brighter red and Carla batted her eyes at her, stroking her tail on Nellie's dress.

By the time she finished, the cream towel was black with grime and the water a dull gray; Nellie was red and almost panting, fanning at herself with a paper fan.

Butternut skin washed smooth and clean, a nude Carla sashayed towards Nellie. "I want to thank you properly," Carla said in a low, husky almost-growl.

A knock sounded on the door and Carla wanted to curse. Nellie's eyes grew wide, and she shooed Carla behind the door.

"Miss Hanson? Mr. Rogerson is here to see you." The housekeeper said, cracking open the door.

"I'm sorry," Nellie panted, moving into the open doorway. Her face and neck were flushed, and she was fanning herself furiously. "Please tell Mr. Rogerson that I'm indisposed. Womanly," Nellie gulped and her eyes glanced at Carla, fell to her rounded breasts with their black, erect nipples. "Problems." She whispered.

"Alright, I'll tell him." There was disapproval in the housekeeper's words, but she bustled away as Nellie clicked the door shut.

Carla moved forward and cupped Nellie's chin, bringing her mouth up to meet her lips. Nellie hesitated at first, stiff as a board. Carla put her arms around Nellie's shoulders and pulled her closer. Nellie responded, moving her lips against Carla's, relaxing against her. Soft down feathers tickled Carla's face as Nellie wrapped her hands around Carla's butt and stroked the base of Carla's tail. Carla gasped in pleasure, arching her back and pulling away.

They fell together back onto the bed with Nellie on top. Nellie's skirts tangled around Carla's legs as Nellie massaged the base of her tail. Carla writhed under the tingling spasms jolting up her back. The longer feathers on Nellie's neck brushed her teeth.

"Don't stop," Carla cried as Nellie pulled away.

"Shh!" Nellie gestured at the door. "Help me get this off," She whispered, reaching around herself to tug at the back lacing of the gown.

"Oh, I will." Carla rolled to the side, pulling Nellie with her. She grabbed Nellie's hand and placed it on her breast, then kissed her hard. Nellie's grip tightened and Carla moaned into her mouth. While Nellie rolled her breast between her fingers Carla reached behind Nellie, fumbling with the laces.

Nellie pulled away from Carla, breathing hard. "You must get behind me to get them off."

Carla pushed up and straddled Nellie's back, grinding her private bits into Nellie's bottom as she unlaced Nellie's corset. Nellie giggled.

Once the corset strings were loose, Nellie sat up and pulled it off, before Carla helped her out of the dress, careful not to catch any of Nellie's feathers on the lace.

"You have wings!" Carla gasped, marveling at the feathers that draped from Nellie's arms. The dress had hidden the full, marvelous extent of Nellie's feathers. "I wish." Nellie blushed and lay back on the bed, spreading herself out and open. "I can't fly with them."

The end of Carla's tail twitched and her ears cocked as she crawled overtop of Nellie. "I can help you fly."

As Carla leaned into kiss her, Nellie turned her head away, biting her lower lip. "Carla, I... I've never had sexual relations with anyone. What if I-"

Carla flicked her tail up and stroked it across Nellie's face. "I'll be gentle; I promise you'll enjoy this."

10

"But will you?" Nellie squeezed her eyes shut, biting down harder on her lip.

"I already am." Carla smiled and licked Nellie's neck. Nellie shivered and moaned as Carla moved down to her collarbone. Her soft tongue lapped at Nellie's feathers. They were softer even than they looked, sliding like water against her skin. Small down feathers, like those on Nellie's face, covered her breasts and belly down to her cleft. Carla rubbed her cheeks, nose, and furry ears across the small opalescent mounds of Nellie's bosom, enjoying the feathers ruffling her skin and fur. Nellie reached a hand up and grasped Carla's long black hair as Carla blew a breath out against Nellie's erect nipple.

Carla reached down to rub at Nellie's privates and found it dripping. She rubbed a finger over Nellie's nub as she sucked on her nipple until Nellie arched and moaned. Then, she kissed lower, still gently rubbing, until her mouth took over for her finger.

Nellie let out a soft moan and spasmed under her, clutching at the rumbled bedcover. "Oh, Carla! More!"

They lay together in the bed, kissing and fondling, taking turns on each other, until the light faded. When they grew tired, they spooned together under the covers, although Carla continued to rub her tail across Nellie's feathered legs, delighting in their softness.

A soft knock at the door roused Carla from her light slumber. She always had been a light sleeper, wakening at the slightest sound. Next to her Nellie stirred, but didn't wake.

"Miss Hanson? I have supper for you. Soup and bread, to help your pains," the housekeeper said from the other side of the door.

Carla gently shook Nellie until she snorted awake. She smiled up at Carla and leaned up to kiss her.

"Miss Hanson?"

Nellie pulled away and Carla stifled a twinge of loss. This had been the best sex she'd ever had, but it was not to be. Tomorrow Carla would go back to the streets and Nellie would marry.

"Leave the tray by the door. I'll retrieve it in a moment," Nellie called as she slid out of bed and turned on the oil lamp on the end table. She walked naked to her wardrobe for a robe.

Carla put her head on her hands, admiring the way Nellie's feathers almost seemed to glow in the gaslight as she pulled on a plush robe.

They shared dinner in between kisses, and the rest of the night they spent enjoying each other's bodies. In the morning, after another shared meal, Carla broke the news to Nellie.

"I must go. If your housekeeper finds me here, you'll be in trouble," Carla said. They lay naked; tangled together in the sheets.

"Must you leave so soon?" Nellie bit her lip, lashes glistening with unshed tears. "But those men-"

"Have turned their search elsewhere, I'm sure. Clean, with a disguise, I can blend into the crowds. Perhaps even find a job, get off the streets."

Nellie gulped and took Carla's hand. "Come back, tonight?"

Carla hesitated. "I'll try."

Climbing down from the balcony was harder than coming up had been, mostly because Carla was trying to keep Nellie's gown clean and tear-free as she went.

The pre-dawn air was chilly on the exposed skin of her neck and chest, but Carla hardly noticed. She went about most of the day in a daze. Her day and night with Nellie didn't seem real in the harsh light of day, yet it was all she could think about. That evening her feet seemed to walk herself back to Nellie's mansion, where Nellie was waiting in the garden.

That night again was magical and the next. During the day Carla found work at a fancy shop; Nellie's fancy gifted dress had opened doors that Carla hadn't even known existed. Each night she visited Nellie, losing more of herself to Nellie's infectious smile.

"What would you do, if you weren't to marry Mr. Rogerson?" Carla asked as they lay cuddled together after a particularly sweet lovemaking session.

"I don't know." Nellie sighed, reaching up to pet one of Carla's pointed ears.

"No ideas at all?" Carla teased. "Nothing excites you?"

"Well, it's a bit embarrassing." She flushed red.

"I'm sure it's wonderful." Carla sat up on the bed, crossing her legs. "I always wanted to see the world. Did you know I've never left London?"

"The Americas." Nellie's face lit up, eyes alight with inner fire. "I met some Americans at the Great Expo. They were from the Wild West and showed off their new clockwork steam engine. It sounded so exciting!" Her face fell again. "But father and Mr. Rogerson would never approve."

"Let's go!" Carla leaned over, unsure where this sudden idea had come from. But now that it was there, it wouldn't leave. "Run away, together, tonight, just the two of us. I've been saving my money, I bet I have enough for passage on a steamer ship-"

"I can't, Carla love." Nellie didn't look over at her as she spoke, but there was regret in her voice. "I've duties here."

"Duties that will make you unhappy. Come with me, we can go anywhere. Or everywhere." Carla looked away, already knowing the answer. In the mirror, Nellie's reflection shook its head.

"They are my duties. I cannot be reckless."

Carla ran her hand through Nellie's hair. "Is it not more reckless to marry a man you dislike?"

Nellie sat up and silenced Carla with a long kiss. When she pulled away tears glistened on her face. "I love you, Carla, but I have obligations, duties..."

"I can't keep going on like this. Sneaking about, stolen kisses. You're all I can think about." Carla began to cry.

"Shhh..." Nellie pulled her into her arms. "After I marry I'll get you a job in my husband's house. Then we can see each other every day-"

"See you, but not touch you. Not talk like we do now. Then see you go into his room at night? No, I can't." Carla wiped her face, hating herself even as the words tumbled from her lips. "This will be our last night together."

Nellie bit her lip, tears streaming down her face. "Then let's make it a memorable one."

The next morning a banging on the front door woke Carla and Nellie. Carla's eyes widened as she saw the sun. "I overslept!" She whispered in horror as she gathered her dress. She gave Nellie a quick kiss on the cheek before slipping into her dress.

"Miss Nellie," the housekeeper said from Nellie's door. "Time to get up."

As she made her way to the balcony, Nellie's door opened, and the housekeeper that Carla had glimpsed her first morning here bustled through.

The housekeeper shrieked and flailed. "Intruder!"

Carla darted for the railing, but the old housekeeper was faster than she looked. She grabbed the back of Carla's dress and hung on, screaming for help. Carla twisted kicking at the housekeeper's arm while Nellie threw a robe over her nakedness.

As Carla pulled free, the back of the dress tearing with a savage rip, a middle-aged man in a dapper suit appeared in Nellie's door. "What's going on?" His eyes widened as he took in Nellie, skin showing through the gaps in the robe, Carla in her torn dress, and the hysterical housekeeper.

Carla cringed, knowing what was coming next. Nellie's father would call the Bobbies, and she'd be back at the workhouse before lunch.

"Everyone, calm down." Nellie pulled her robe closed and pointed at Carla. "She isn't an intruder; she is a friend."

Carla relaxed a fraction of an inch.

"But, Miss!" Mrs. Norwood protested. "She's a blooming thief, a cat burglar. She's wearing one of your old dresses that went missing a few months ago, and your pearls."

"I gave them to her, as gifts." Nellie didn't miss a beat. Carla straightened and did her best to pull her torn dress closed.

"A friend? Who visits before dawn? And doesn't announce herself to the housekeeper." Mr. Hansen glared at Carla. "You're covering for her. Mrs. Norwood, lock this thief in the pantry while I send a runner for the Bobbies."

Carla paced as much as she was able in the small confines of the kitchen pantry. She'd already tried the door, hoping against hope that her meager lock picking skills would be enough, but it was barred from the outside. The small room had no exits, she was trapped.

Her tail twitched as she walked, two steps, spin, two steps, and back again, but Carla couldn't see any way out. It didn't matter, anyway. Freedom or the workhouse, neither life included Nellie in it.

Light footsteps scuffled across the tiles outside. Not a Bobby. They clomped in their heavy boots, confident in their status as bullies and toughs. Carla stopped and faced the door, ears perking with curiosity. A familiar scent hit her nostrils. Nellie?

The bar scrapped and the door creaked open. Nellie's face appeared in the gap, holding a finger across her lips. Carla slipped out of the opening, and stopped, shocked at Nellie's dress.

She wore a young man's suit, too long in the legs and tight on her hips and chest, which was curiously flat. Her long locks were hidden under a wide bowler hat and she carried a large Gladstone bag.

"What are you wearing?" Carla whispered.

"A disguise." She grinned and twirled. "I have one here for you, too." She held out an arm, which had more men's clothing draped over it.

Carla couldn't help but smile back and quickly pulled off her torn dress. As Carla picked up the shirt Nellie came up behind her with a length of bandage.

"To hide your chest."

Carla bobbed her head at the bag. Carla's cat-like curiosity burned over its contents. "What's in there?"

Nellie clicked the top open and angled it so Carla could see inside. Stacks of English bills filled it to the brim.

Nellie grinned. "My dowry. To finance our trip to the Wild West."

That night a pair of gentlemen booked passage on the new Trans-Atlantic airship service to the Americas. They made an odd pair as they walked up the gangplank to the passenger galley together, a black cat-hybrid and a swan-hybrid, wearing ill-fitting matching suits. But both grinned, brimming with excitement as they talked about their trip around the world and the adventures that awaited them together.

The Monster in the Mist

This story was originally published in *Dogs of War Volume 1* edited by Fred Patten and released by Furplanet in Jan 2017.

Wet grass soaked through Isok's hunting leathers. The damp fur itched and more rain continued to drip slowly on him as it filtered down through the cracked brown foliage above. Figured, first rain in months and it had to happen on his first hunt as a full member of the pack. He flicked his ears, scattering water droplets onto the black-furred hunters next to him.

<Be patient, young pup,> the hunt leader gefired to him. The mind to mind communication was handy for hunting, allowing the pack to communicate without startling any potential prey.

A flash of brown fur through the leaves drew his attention back to the reason they were here. The dry season had been longer and dryer than normal and it had come after a particularly cold and snow-free winter. The herds of deer, their normal prey, had been hit hard by the abnormally cold weather and most of the new fawns hadn't survived. As the summer wore on and the streams, rivers, and even lakes had dried to mere trickles the herds migrated away in search of food and water. The current drizzle Isok suffered under was the first in many moons.

<Steady.>

Isok pulled his back paws up and settled them firmly into the mud, digging in his back claws. His front paws gripped his spear tight enough that he had to relax, lest his front claws ruin the shaft.

<Strike!>

As one the pack charged from their hiding spots to converge on an undersized boar. Its back still showed the ghost of baby spots and it was so thin its hide was pulled taunt over bones. Before Isok could throw his own spear one of his pack mate's hit the beast right in the eye. The boar squealed loud and high, making Isok wince. It took two steps and then collapsed on its side, blood dripping from its eye socket and the back of its neck where the rock spear tip poked through the fur.

The pack circled the dead boar. Isok dropped his spear and fell to all fours, pushing at the loam around him with the tip of his muzzle. No other fresh spore. Underneath the top layer of brown leaves was the faint scent of the rest of the sounder, but the track was days old. This juvenile must have gotten separated; unable to keep up it was left behind to fend for itself.

Boar were good eating and usually a single boar could feed half the clan for several nights. But this one was so thin Isok guessed might feed two adult clan members for a single day.

The hunt leader, Rahil, cocked his head at Isok as he retrieved his spear and climbed to his feet. Isok's ears and tail fell and he lowered his head, looking up at Rahil. "No others. The trail is old. This one was left behind."

Rahil snarled without teeth and stalked over to lecture the other two hunters about proper skinning techniques. Isok relaxed slightly.

Howling rose up from the forest around them. Isok's ear's stood straight up and he whirled, raising his muzzle to sniff the air. The wind shifted revealing intruders hiding nearby. He recognized the scent immediately, although a compelling undertone to it had him oddly at ease. "Comet Clan!" he yelled, warning the others.

"Protect the kill!"

The battle was over in less time than it took Isok to be knocked flat on his back by a Comet Clan attacker. When Isok recovered Rahil was lying before the Comet Clan chief, a spear sticking out of the back of his shoulder. The other two Bright Moon Clan hunters were held captive by three spear-wielding warriors.

Isok shifted, taking his eyes off the hair-raising sight of a spear a claw length from the curve of his throat long enough to look up at his own captor. The most exquisite female he'd ever seen growled down at him. Silky mahogany fur covered her back from the tip of her tail all the way to the delicate curve of her muzzle where her lips peeled up over gleaming fangs. The color faded to fawn on her throat and stomach, the downy fuzz interrupted only by a leather loincloth strung about her hips.

His tongue lolled from his muzzle as he leaned his head up as far as he dared and inhaled the rich musky scent of her. A pin-prick of pain on his windpipe only heightened his growing lust.

"Stay."

The command, said in the sharp bark of an Alpha, snapped him out of his trance. The Comet Alpha scowled down at him. "Keep away from my daughter."

Even his growling stomach couldn't keep the Comet Alpha's daughter from his mind during the long trek back to the Bright Moon's encampment. Rahil noticed his distraction and guessing the obvious source tried to lecture Isok about his duties to Clan and pack. Famines were not the time to start a family. Especially not with a female from a waring Clan. The words made sense when Rahil said them, but the meaning rolled away when he caught a whiff of her scent clinging to his fur.

When the first Clan members spotted them the greeting howls were excited. However, when the scouts noticed that the hunters didn't have a fresh kill with them, and that Rahil had a bloody bandage around his arm the howls were subdued and tinged with worry.

By the time they trudged into the main camp it was to snarls and turned backs. Isok spotted his litter mate peeking at them around the curve of a yurt. When he met her gaze she narrowed her eyes and turned away. Isok sighed. He couldn't blame his sister in the least as he was very conscious of his own gnawing hunger.

The Alpha met them in the center of the camp, standing on the dry, cracked dirt. It seemed the drizzle that had haunted their hunt hadn't reached this far. The hunting party came to a stop in front of the

Alpha, unconsciously arranging themselves in a line with Rahil at the lead. Isok knelt, lifted his head, and turned his muzzle, presenting his neck to the Alpha.

Rahil knelt as well, although he didn't give as much neck as Isok. Even from behind Isok could see the tension in Rahil's posture and smell the blood soaking through the bandages.

"You are injured. Yet you have no meat, no kill."

"Yes, Alpha. We did have a kill. Comet clan ambushed us." So few words, but they summed up the situation perfectly.

The Alpha lifted his head and bayed. Ears perked up all over camp and immediately clan members rushed into the circle. Most of the clan were already close, having come in hopes that this hunt had been successful. In less time than Isok would have thought possible the circle filled. Almost a hundred Jegera stood in hopeful silence, waiting for the Alpha's words about how he was going to save them.

Isok stood and moved back towards the edge of the crowd with the rest of the youths, making room for the oldest and wisest to gather closer to the Alpha.

The Alpha took a deep breath. The crowd trembled in anticipation, ears high and tails wagging slowly. "Another hunt come to naught."

"We must go north!" One of the young females cried. In the press of the crowd Isok couldn't see who. He shuddered. North, where the mist monsters lived in the cracks of the mountains?

"That way lies the Yaka," the Alpha said, "and the danger is too great. This has been debated before and always reason won out."

"My puppy died last night. Starved to death. Is a Yaka any greater of a threat?" Now Isok had a face to put to the voice. Only one female had given birth to a live litter this spring. Isok had played stick with the pups before he'd left on the hunt. They'd hardly had the energy to move. Nothing but skin over bones with distended stomachs and fat puppy faces.

"We've already moved farther north than we ever have in this clan's history, following what remains of the herds towards the distant peaks."

Not so distant now. From the campsite it was hidden, but in the meadow down by the stream you could see a snow capped mountain top. The herd's trail had continued north towards it, but the Alpha had camped them here, too afraid of the mist monster legends to allow the Clan to travel any farther.

"And now we have word that the Comet Clan has followed us here."

Someone whimpered and Isok wrinkled his nose at the scent of urine as one of the pups cowered in fear. A sign of how violent it had gotten before the Bright Moon Clan had marched north, when the Yaka incited less fear than a rival clan.

The memory of the Comet female's musk caressed his nose and he panted, too hot. His fur itched and he suppressed an irritated snarl when the pup next to him thumped him with a careless swing of his tail.

He couldn't deny it any longer. The beginnings of mating frenzy. Over her. A Comet. Only mating with his Chosen would end his torment. But with their Clans at war over the scarce prey the Alpha would never allow him a chance to win over his daughter.

If only there was a way to solve both problems.

The Alpha stood, his barrel chest drawing every eye. "The will of the pack has been heard and weighed. Leaving our traditional territory was a mistake, perhaps. But neither will we proceed north. Hunting has been better here than it has been anywhere else this summer. We stay until first snow."

Although that had been his first time on a hunting pack, he had seen the rest of the hunters come back and most of them returned empty-pawed and tired. Younger and younger pups were being sent with the hunters, on the theory that more hunters had more chance of success. Isok didn't believe that. More inexperienced hunters would merely drive off the prey, if there was even any to find.

The Comet Clan female would only be his if everyone had enough food that there was no reason to fight. No reason to deny his request to woo a female of another clan. When he was growing up, before the drought started he remembered an older sibling of his going off to join another clan.

There were complications though. Jegera were pack hunters and he didn't know how to hunt alone. Surely a few of the others around his age felt the same. Isok noted who complained the loudest about the decision to stay. The younger pups, like him, were surer bets. By the time he stumbled into bed the sun had crested the horizon and he had made up his mind.

In the end only two others agreed to join him in his northward hunt for prey. It would have to be enough.

That night they planned and packed, gathering what few supplies they could find. Each of them packed a small hunting pannier with only the bare essentials. A blanket for each of them, several filled water-skins, a stone knife that Adlie snuck out of her father's hunting kit, and Isok's spear. After a short discussion they decided not to bring any food with them. The pack needed it more, and if they right about their trip they'd they soon find prey aplenty.

The sun rose and the camp quieted down until only the early morning bird songs could be heard. Jegera didn't usually start to stir until the late afternoon, waking as the heat of the day faded away. While their night vision was excellent, most Jegera had trouble with bright light. So it was that the three pups padded softly away, their absence unremarked. They easily avoided the day guard, who was there mostly to scare off intruders and other predators rather than stop Clan members from leaving the area.

The chance of someone coming after them was low. Resources were too scarce and hunters needed too desperately to hunt prey rather than chase foolish pups into the legendary northern mountains.

Isok pushed them hard, stopping only for needed bathroom and water breaks. His four legs were trembling with hunger and fatigue when he finally allowed them to stop as the sun began to set.

Many other predators hunted at night and Isok didn't want to be caught unawares in unfamiliar territory. Better to wait a while and grow familiar with this strange northern forest's night life before moving on. While they waited Isok watched the trees swaying in the wind. Instead of leaves these northern trees had needles for branches, so sharp enough to draw the blood of the unwary. These forests had more dangers than just those on four legs.

Deep shadows mixed with the remaining sunlight to form swirling clouds of impenetrable darkness. A rustling in the bushes had all three of them on their feet, claws out and lips pulled back in silent snarls. Adlie charged while Isok stood frozen with indecision.

<Foolish,> a warm voice sounded in their heads. Adlie slid to a stop, her tail lowered and one ear twitching in confusion. <Haven't you hunted before?>

"Who's there?" Isok growled, pushing in front of Adlie. Garor, the third member of their small band, cowered behind him, the stone knife clutched tightly in his front paws. Isok could distinctly smell his fear.

The vision of loveliness that was the Comet Alpha's daughter stepped out of the bushes, ears erect and tail high. Her spear hung from one relaxed paw. She smiled at Adlie without teeth, and then turned her attention to Isok.

Twilight sun sparkled in her fur as she crouched and gently set her spear down in the leaf mulch. Her nostrils flared when Isok took a step forward. Her scent filled the clearing and he inhaled deeply. This close the mating frenzy struggled to take hold of him and he had to fight to keep his gaze on her face. She licked her muzzle, the pink tongue bright against her dark fur. Isok almost lost it. A gulp and a whine escaped him before he was able to address her.

"What-" another lungful of her musk scattered his thoughts. "What, why, here-"

"I think what Isok means is why are you here, Comet Bitch?" Adlie shifted up to a crouch and bared her claws.

"The same reason as you, I suppose," she said, ears flicking about to indicate the woods around them. "Hunting."

"Alone?" Isok cocked his head.

"Um…"

"I knew it, you followed me." Isok wagged his tail and straightened, lolling his tongue at her.

"Don't," she barked.

"What's your name?" Isok asked at the same time Adlie said, "Who are you?"

"To answer both your questions, I am Henra, daughter of the Comet Alpha." Henra returned Isok's slobbering smile with one of her own, nostrils flaring again.

"Why are you here then, if not to help us?" Adlie cocked her head, looking back and forth between Henra and Isok. "Wait." She crouched and approached Isok, nose in the air then did the same to Henra who pined her ears back at the approach but made no move to stop the small female. "Mating smell." She shook her head. "I smell it on you both. Isok is right, you did follow him."

"Fine, I did," Henra growled back. "So now tell me why the three of you are out here. Mist monsters hunt these woods, you know."

"Hunting." Garor finally got up his courage and stepped forward to join their conversation. "Somewhere the Comet Clan hasn't already cleared out." He snorted at Henra in derision.

Henra huffed and retrieved her spear, then pointed up through the trees into the growing darkness. "The Comet clan is smart enough to stay away."

"Monsters' aren't real," Isok said, clearing a space on the ground and settling down to his haunches. The other three shot wary glances at each other before joining him.

Henra sat farthest away, almost at the edge of the clearing, while Garor and Adlie settled down next to him.

"Then where did the legends come from," Henra said after everyone had settled, waving a languid paw around her head. "Not from air."

The last bits of twilight faded away as the group sat, quietly staring at each other. Even before the drought Comet Clan and Bright Moon Clan hadn't gotten along and Isok was doubly intimidated by Henra's intense stare.

He distracted himself by searching the brightening stars for familiar constellations and trying to determine which way was north. When he looked back down feelers of mist were rolling in from the trees. One crawled over his outstretched tail, giving him the chills.

Isok stood quickly, backing away from the oncoming mist in a crouch. Without taking his eyes off the ground he reached around behind himself and pulled his spear free of the ties on his pannier. Eyes wide, Garor and Adlie did the same. Henra, closest to the trees, was already almost lost in the mist. Isok could barely see her ear tips poking up through it. She stood up on four legs, sending the mist swirling away. Her face was unreadable as she stiffly marched towards them.

Adlie whispered from somewhere behind him. "Mist always proceeds the appearance of the Yaka in the legend."

Garor growled his agreement.

"Superstitious nonsense," Henra muttered as she moved up next to them. Her tail was sticking straight back, as if she fought to keep it from curling between her legs and her ears were quivering.

"Be brave," Isok whimpered to himself. He turned and looked at his small pack's faces. He'd started this expedition and as the pack leader he needed to be brave for them. Isok slipped the spear back into its straps and straightened up onto two legs, towering over the other three who still stood on four. The Bright Moon alpha always used this move to great effect.

Isok cleared his throat and began again. "Henra is right." His voice seemed to disappear into the encroaching mist. "We three came here because we didn't believe the legends. Don't let a little mist spook you into forgetting our purpose."

"Oh, little pup," a voice hissed from the darkness. The mist deadened the sound and made it impossible for Isok to locate the source. "Sometimes the Legends are true."

Garor let out an ear-splitting howl and fled into the trees, kicking up dirt and lichen in his wake.

"Garor," Isok called after him, unwilling to following him and leave Adlie and Henra alone with the voice. Only terrified howling answered him, the sound getting quieter until it faded away to silence. Isok spun, eyes probing the thick mist and analyzing the shadows in the trees, searching for the intruder. He even looked up, into the branches, but nothing was there.

"Well now, too brave to follow your little friend back to safety? Too foolish not to run when given the chance."

A shape materialized out of the mist, sketched in darkness. Isok could only see an outline and strain as he might no details presented themselves. It had tall pointed ears, wide shoulders, and an outline fuzzed by fur; it stood on all fours, facing the pups head on. Isok gulped when he realized that the beasts eyes, or where the eyes would be if Isok could see them, where level with his own, despite the fact that he stood on tall on two legs and the beast on four.

30

"Who are you?" His voice barely trembled as he struggled to contain the fear that was causing his heart to almost beat out of his chest. He could smell the terror stink coming off Adlie and Henra, and knew he too must reek of it, but he wouldn't let the beast have the satisfaction of hearing his fear as well as smelling it. There was another scent, too, of another Jegera but it was faint and all but drowned out by the fear stink coming off the group.

"Insolent pup, to come into another's home and demand." The shape moved forward, growing larger as it came. Details swirled up out of the mist. No, it was the mist swirling up to add definition to the shape. A shape made up of the mist itself. Eyes opened, white on black, and Isok could see the outline of trees through them.

"We mean no disrespect, honored Yaka." Isok knelt down and presented his throat to the shape, like he had for the Bright Moon Alpha less than a day ago.

The shape flickered. Was it so surprised by his move?

Isok stood flicking his ears to rid it of the night-time biting insects and stepped forward. "We apologize for our trespass, but we were desperate. Our streams are dry and barren, our hunting grounds empty of prey."

"Very well." The voice boomed louder, seeming to rattle the very bones in Isok's skull with the force of its proclamation. "You may hunt in our lands tonight only, insolent-yet-polite pup. And only for *hukra.*"

Isok exchanged a glance with Henra, who looked as puzzled as he felt. His ears skewed in confusion. "Honored Yaka, we know not of these *hukra* you speak of."

The mist form turned, dissipating slowly back into the night. "Go north, then east. You will find a river.

31

Follow it upstream." The mist slithered away and vanished almost as quickly as it had come.

"We must go inform the Alpha, so that he can send real hunters!" Adlie stamped a back leg and lowered her head, turning away from Isok and Henra as if ashamed.

"You know he won't." Isok let the outburst go unpunished. He wasn't an Alpha, or even a leader, to do such things.

Adlie plopped her butt down on the ground and stared morosely at her front paws, curling and uncurling the claws into the dirt. "I know."

"These hukra, though." Henra paced on all fours, tail swishing thoughtfully behind her as she circled them. "We don't know anything about them. The Yaka could be sending us into a trap."

Isok shook his head and licked his lips, imaging he could already taste the meat on his tongue. The others had to be convinced to continue.

"In the Legends the Yaka can kill with the mist. If it wanted us dead -" He left the thought unfinished when Adlie cringed and pulled her tail around her front paws.

"Isok has a point," Henra said, still pacing. "But then, why tell us of these hukra creatures?"

"Perhaps they have some protection against the Yaka?" Isok, tired of trying to keep his eyes on a pacing Henra, turned his eyes to Adlie. "But it really doesn't matter. The hukra are food, the Clans are starving."

"Let's go then." Henra started off north. Isok trotted after her, wondering when he'd lost control of this expedition. A night breeze blew Henra's scent back to him and he realized he didn't care.

After several claw marks of walking, the quarter moon had risen high in the sky. They'd reached the stream and now followed it upstream, as directed.

The trees were thick along the banks and going slow. By the time they arrived at the place where the hukra herd slept the moon was beginning to set.

What little moonlight remained glittered on hard carapaces and thick horns, longer than a Jegera was tall. The hukra, in a word, were huge and armored beasts. The entire herd was spread out in the meadow by the stream; about a dozen individuals of varying sizes. Even the smallest, half hidden behind the bulk of what Isok guessed was its mama, was probably ten tail lengths in height - a good three tail lengths taller than Isok himself standing on two legs.

<We need a plan,> Henra gefired him and Adlie as they slipped back into the woods. While the breeze was light, it was there and Isok was satisfied to see Henra move them until they stood downwind from the herd.

<I see a newborn one.> Isok relayed its position in the herd to the others. The moonlight and their night vision washed the color out of things, so he hadn't been able to guess age or sex of the other creatures, but small was good. Easier, he figured. In their deer hunting the small were protected...unless they fell behind. Then they were easy prey for a trained pack. Which they weren't.

"I have a plan," Henra gefired them the basic idea. Isok was impressed. It could just work.

Isok volunteered for the most dangerous part; Henra's smell drove out all reason and he needed to impress the strong-willed Alpha's daughter. While Isok circled around the unfamiliar woods he began to regret his bravado. He hoped Henra was suitably impressed.

Unfamiliar night birds trilled in the trees above him. Isok reached the north end of the meadow and crouched. From this angle he could fully see the baby hukra, sleeping leaned against one of the massive adults. Now that he had time while he waited for Adlie and Henra's signal he studied the animals.

Even this baby had armored plates running along its back. It had probably recently had a growth spurt, as there were big gaps between the plates that weren't there on the adult creatures. In addition, the horns were rounded little nubs on the nose and forehead instead of the wicked looking monstrosities the adults wielded.

<We are ready.>

Isok abandoned his analysis and lopped out of the trees towards the baby. He tried to stay away from the hukra's horned heads, but otherwise didn't try to hide his scent. This kill wasn't about stealth; plus the more he thought about it the more he realized these beasts wouldn't have a reason to fear Jegeran musk yet.

After he'd gone a few tree lengths into the clearing, Isok worked his spear free of the pannier on his back. If he was thinking he'd have gotten it ready while he was waiting. A snoring hukra shifted its weight somewhere behind him, and the ground trembled. The spear dropped from nerveless paw. "It's sleeping and it still scares me half to death," he muttered as he retrieved the dropped spear.

The baby hukra was only a bit away from him now, although Isok would have to circle around one more adult to get a clear shot. Unfortunately when he padded around the adults back he discovered that about three of them had bunch up together in a line. He'd have to risk standing by the head, because there wasn't a way around.

He walked back the way he'd come and inched around the beast's muzzle, between it and another hukra's backside. It was tight but he got through without touching any of them. Not thinking he wagged his tail. He felt the fur brush across something warm and froze, instinctively dropping down to the ground. The grass in the meadow had been crushed flat by hukra feet and he felt exposed just lying in the dirt. A snort, a beast very close stomped a foot rattling Isok's skull. His heart felt like it would burst from his chest, but nothing else happened.

He whispered a small prayer to the Moon God for watching over three foolish pups and then a second to thank the God for this opportunity of promise. As quietly as he could he climbed to two legs, crouched and balanced the spear the way he'd been taught. The baby's side was a broad target - he couldn't miss, really- but he needed to hit between the two plates on the neck. This would only work if the baby was mortally injured or not able to keep up with the rest of the herd. He lunged forward, snapping his arm and releasing the spear.

The spear flew straight and true, striking the young armored monster right between the two ill-fitting plates on its neck. It let out a deep wail and charged forward, running into the side of the other hukra directly in front of it. Isok had been expecting this and he was already charging forward, evading a stomping foot as the adult the baby had struck reared back in shock. Isok leapt up using the powerful muscles in his leg to thrust himself as far off the ground as he was able, then grabbed the baby creatures protruding back plate with his claws and pulled himself up and over - like a game of leapfrog over a giant boulder.

Around him the herd awoke to panic and confusion. The adults began to stampede away from the river and into the trees, driven by Adlie and Henra's snapping jaws. Saplings and smaller trees cracked audibly, the sound loud even over the bellows of the panicking monsters. Isok hung onto his prize as the baby ran with the herd, blood spraying from its neck.

The smell of blood followed the stampeding herd, adding to the frenzy and confusion. Just as they reached the tree line, and Isok began to panic. Perhaps his strike had not been as true as he thought; the baby collapsed under him with one final spasm. Isok held on, digging his claws into the tender skin between the plates. The baby bucked and writhed, while tree-sized monsters streamed past. It reminded him of nightmares he'd had in the past, and would have thought this too a dream except that the dust and debris kicked up by their massive three-toed feet clogged his throat and nose. Finally it was over and the bellowing faded into the distance.

The night was silent again, if only for a few moments. While Isok hung onto the now still-baby, willing his reluctant claws to re-sheath and trembling with unspent adrenalin, the normal sounds of the forest gradually returned. Night-birds trilled, small creatures rustled through the whirlwind of mess left by the stampede; in the distance something big roared its domination over that part of the woods. Isok remembered how to breathe by the time Adlie and Henra found him still clinging to the massive baby's side like a bur.

"Well, that was a little more dramatic than I intended," Henra remarked dryly. Her body language was aloof, tail in a neutral position ears not quite perked. But her smell, Isok felt himself responding and this time - with a month's worth of fresh meat underneath him and the tang of blood in the air - he didn't fight it.

Adlie's ears went back and she wrinkled her muzzle and trotted off. "Don't stop on my account," she growled at them as she disappeared into the underbrush. Isok hardly noted her absence.

"Henra," Isok said as he hopped off the baby hukra's side and landed lightly on the ground. He felt like he was walking through air he felt so lite. "Be my mate."

In response Henra tackled him to the ground, licking his muzzle while Isok ripped off her loincloth. He took her right then and there, the blood only feeding their mating frenzy.

After Isok and Henra were satiated and Adlie had returned they started work on carving up the kill for transport. Which was harder than they realized it was going to be after they discovered the Garor had fled with their only knife.

Luckily their claws were sharp, and after filling their bellies with the rich brains, heart and liver they had plenty of energy for the task. Isok couldn't get enough of watching Henra move in the starlight, her eyes sparkling each time he caught her gaze.

After dark they started the long walk back to camp. Adlie still feared the Yaka, but Isok didn't think they had anything to worry about now. Just after the moon rose they were traveling downstream, their bellies full and their packs heavy.

The mist came as it had before, seeming to seep out of the ground itself. On the trail in front of them the great creature rose up from the fog, eyes glowing red, its mouth opened in a toothy grin.

Isok stepped forward, averting his eyes and presenting his throat with no little fear. No matter his thoughts during the day, the Yaka's very presence cowered him. But Henra and Adlie depended on him, he would be strong for his new mate and pack member. "We found the hukra creatures, scared them away, and slew one of their young."

A scent wafted to him, the same Jegera he'd smelled before, but this time their fear was less, bolstered by their success. Isok lifted his nose to the air, trying to place the location of the spy.

"Better than I expected from you." The Yaka's form grew wispy for a moment before solidifying once more. "But I see from your thoughts you plan to leave, come back with more of your kind."

Henra gave Isok a wide-eyed look and he could feel Adlie shaking behind him. "We do, merciful Yaka." His voice shook and he gulped bending low and inclining his head even further.

The Yaka roared, they cry shaking the trees. A flock of birds startled out of sleep, erupted from a nearby bush in a flurry of wings and beaks before shooting away up towards the stars.

"Honored Yaka," Isok said, lowering so far his belly touched the ground. Not weak, he had to keep telling himself, merely submitting to a powerful capacious alpha-monster who can pluck the thoughts from head and grind my bones to dust. "Without the food provided by the hukra our clans will starve."

"And if you allow us to hunt the hukra, there will be less of them around to bother you." Henra said, moving up beside Isok and scrapping down low beside him. "After all, why else would you have us hunt them for you unless you cannot kill them yourself."

Isok risked a look up, getting a muzzle full of leaf muck on the tip of his nose while doing so. The Yaka's form had shrunk a bit and had gotten wispy at the edges again. In fact, it had faded so much that where once had been only the vague outline of trees through the insubstantial form now where stark poles crisp against the darker background. And there, within the fading mist, Isok thought he saw a small shape standing where the Yaka had been. A sample of the air told him the strange Jegera was also standing close to that same spot. Bah, a phantom not at all.

His legs pulled up under him, claws gripping the dirt he pushed off straight at the form wavering through the mist. It wasn't the best jumping tackle he'd ever done, but it was enough. He slammed into the side of the form, felt warm flesh and fur beneath him as he hit. A high pitched yip sounded from underneath him as they hit the leaf mulch hard. The mist beast popped, like a soap bubble hit with outstretched claw, although the cold mist continued to crawl along his fur there didn't seem to be as much of it as there had been.

They'd landed with Isok on top, and the form he'd hit had been small enough that it was lost underneath him. He sat up, revealing a white-furred Jegera. Unlike his own midnight black fur, short and bristly enough that his dark skin was visible underneath, this pup's white fur was long and soft with a thick undercoat. The pup looked up at him with eyes bluer than a cloudless summer day.

"Get off me, brute!" It was said in the deep voice of the Yaka they'd heard through the mist, although without the almost mystical reverberation it'd had previously.

"What did you do?!" Henra ran up from behind him on all fours. When she saw the white pup she skidded to a stop so fast her back legs lifted off the ground for a moment. "Is that a puppy?"

"I'm not a puppy!" She growled, for this close Isok could smell her. Of mating age, as old as Henra at least.

"You tricked us." Henra sat back on her haunches and began chuckling so hard her sides pressed against the tight straps of her panniers.

"We trick all of you big ones that come up here," the girl growled, pushing Isok's paw away when he reached over to help her stand.

"We?" Isok repeated, still staring at the girl. She smelled like a Jegera, and could probably even pass for one if her fur was shorter and she wasn't so small.

"The Yaka, of course. To keep you Jegera out of our hunting grounds."

"So why send us farther in, to that herd of hukra that you obviously knew was there?" Isok turned to give Adlie a comforting look, but she was gone - vanished into the mist at some point while he and Henra had groveled for the monster that turned out not to be.

"Those armored thugs have been stomping all over the place lately. We can't hunt them, they're too big, and they're scaring away the raop. Plus, when a whole herd of them gets to a stream they turn a pristine watering hole into an unusable muddy mess." A tiny foot stomped on the dirt and Isok had to suppress a giggle at how cute she looked; with her pinned back ears and puffed up tail combined with her wild fur made her look like a end of summer dandelion flower before the wind blew it away.

Henra smiled, tail wagging as she looked down at the little Yaka. "I have a proposition for you-"

The Yaka glared at her. "Go on."

"We," Henra gestured to herself, Isok, and Adlie, "come back with hunters. We live here in the North, and promise only to hunt hukra."

"You will leave a tribute for the Yaka after each hunt." She paused. "And not go past the mountain pass in the north." The Yaka growled, eyes narrowed.

Isok and Henra nodded.

"It's a deal."

Isok, Henra, and Adlie returned to the Bright Moon Clan a few paw-spans before sunset the next day. Between them they had enough meat to feed the hungry villagers for several days, along with tales of great herds roaming the northern mountains. Isok and Henra announced their mating and their plan to form a new Clan in the northern mountains.

Northern Delights

This story was originally published in *ROAR* 8 edited by Mary E. Lowd and released by Furplanet in July 2017.

Rafael walked out of the airport and into a frozen wasteland. Overhead the sky was gray, the sun completely hidden behind the clouds. The wind whistled, sending a swirl of snow down his back. Rafael shivered and pulled up the collar of his bubble-gum pink winter coat. The color hadn't been his first choice, but even in the dead of winter stores in Phoenix didn't exactly carry a large selection of winter wear, especially in sizes that fit a Chihuahua.

He was already cold, and he was only three steps from the warmth of the airport lobby. Rafael scowled and began following the signs towards the taxi cab waiting area. His cell rang, belting out Don Omar singing the first lines of Zumba. *"Pa' este baile no hay salida."*

"You've reached Detective Ferreira," he answered, cutting off the catchy tune. A gray and white

43

barrel-chested malamute walking ahead of him startled and turned to stare down at the little Chihuahua. A lot of people had that reaction when they found out he was a policeman.

"Where are you?" his boss barked at him. The Captain was a pitbull and Rafael could picture him sitting at his desk, jowls quivering with rage, eyes narrowed.

"I'm great, boss, and how are you?" Rafael bared his teeth at the phone and then up at the bigger dog. The malamute blinked and then hurried his steps away.

"I asked where you are detective," his boss repeated, the growl in his voice deepening.

"I'm taking some personal time off, sir. Family emergency." Rafael hung up. The phone rang again, which cut off abruptly when Rafael popped off the back and pulled out the battery.

Rafael jumped into the back of one of the cabs idling at the curb waiting for passengers. The cabbie, a big shaggy thing of indeterminate species, did a double take as Rafael settled into the seat. "What kinda rat are you?"

"The dog kind," Rafael barked back as he snapped on his seat belt.

The cabbie shook his head but hit the 'fare' light on his dash. "Where to?"

"Iditarod starting line," Rafael said and settled back into his seat.

The shaggy dog shrugged and pulled away from the curb. Rafael sat up in his seat, struggling to see out the window. Mostly he could only see the tops of buildings, all covered in snow. Big flakes drifted by the windows.

"Nice jacket," the dog said, grinning at him in the rear-view mirror.

Rafael grinned back at him. "Thanks, it's a family heirloom. You know where the racers wait to start?"

"What, don't tell me you're a competitor?" He howled in laughter.

At this Rafael let out a genuine laugh. "Ha, not hardly. A friend of mine is. Just wanted to wish him luck before he starts."

"A little guy like you? In that crowd? You'll never find him in time. The back area is always a cluster. Best bet is to find a place along the starting stretch and cheer for him as he goes by. I know a good place where the crowd won't be too thick."

Rafael grabbed at the door as the cab made a sudden turn. "Cabron! Watch it. Thing is, I really need to talk to my friend before he starts the race. It's important."

"Your dime. But don't say I didn't warn you." The cabbie pulled over to the curb.

Rafael popped off his seatbelt and stood. Crowds of dogs streamed down the sidewalk outside the cab. In the distance a block ahead of him, almost obscured by falling snow, he could see a flag-topped tower.

"Thanks. Keep the change." Rafael handed the cabbie a twenty before climbing out.

When he opened the door he shivered as the cold air blasted him, seeming to whistle right through his hat and jacket. The snow on the sidewalk crunched under his boots. The sidewalks were shoveled, but more snow was falling all the time. Snow was piled high against the buildings and was ground to slush in the streets beneath the passing car.

Rafael tucked his head down and followed the press of dogs towards the starting line. Either his neon jacket did its job, or the big dogs of Alaska were used to watching for smaller puppies in the press, because no one even came close to stepping on him. But the cabbie had been right about the crowds. Rafael couldn't see anything but furry legs and tails wagging in his face.

"Excuse me, excuse me!" Rafael yelled, trying to get the attention of any of the bigger dogs around him with no avail.

Finally the tide of the crowd spit him out by a long table with a banner across it that read 'Racer Check in.' Arrayed behind it were three big dogs, all northern breeds, like the racers. The area to the left of the table was separated from the crowd by plastic barrier tape.

"Can I help you?" A dark gray malamute glanced at him as Rafael waved a paw about above the tabletop.

Rafael pulled out a glossy photo of a golden furred chow dog and stood on his tiptoes to put it on the table while holding up his Phoenix Police Department badge. "I'm looking for Wang Wei Snelling. He's a racer. It's vitally important I talk to him before he leaves."

"I recognize him. Don't have many chows signed up to race." The malamute handed him the photo back and checked a list in front of her. "The race starts soon, so you have about fifteen minutes to find him. The runners all wait over there. I'll let you through." She then pointed to her left.

"Thanks, ma'am." Rafael wagged his curled tail, already half frozen, and ducked under the tape.

Hundreds of dogs milled about on the other side although his job was made easier by the fact that most of them had white or gray fur. However, his own small size was still a problem. He couldn't see more than a couple of feet through the press. Even worse, loads of backpacks and supplies were piled seemingly at random in the snow blocking his way.

"Excuse me, have you seen this dog?" Rafael held up his photo of Wang Wei and plowed forward into the press, yelling to be heard over the din.

"What the hell are you supposed to be?" said the first dog who noticed him, a towering brown and white Saint Bernard.

"I'm a Chihuahua," Rafael answered him evenly although his hackles rose. "And it's vitally important that I find this dog. His name is Wang Wei and--"

The Bernard cut him off with a loud woof. "Haven't seen him. Now go away, I'm busy."

Rafael shrugged and sidled around the dog and his bags. The next dog, a white Eskimo dog with triangular ears, was a little more polite but knew no more than the first dog. Rafael continued to make his way through the crowd, climbing over luggage and questioning the other racers. Noon was fast approaching and Rafael hadn't gotten any closer to finding Wang Wei.

"Please, sir, have you seen this dog?" The words had long since lost their meaning, but Rafael held up the picture and asked the question.

"Him? Yeah, I have," said a big dog. Rafael wasn't sure but thought he might be some kind of husky.

"Thanks anyway," Rafael said and started to turn away before what the dog had said sunk in. He jerked and spun back. "Wonderful! Can you point me in his direction?" Rafael tucked the photo back into his coat, shivering as he zipped it back up. Even with the coat and hat he was freezing.

"Even better, little guy. I can take you right to him!" The husky mix wagged his tail and gestured.

Rafael fell in beside him, pumping his legs furiously to keep up as the dog took off at a brisk pace through the crowd.

"Thank you so much. You have no idea how important it is that I speak with him." Rafael panted and glanced at his watch. 11:55. He only had a few more minutes before Wang Wei's group was off and running, and then it would be too late.

The husky led him into a ring of three other big dogs. He turned to face Rafael and raised his paws to his sides. "Here we are."

Rafael stopped and blinked in surprise. He glanced around, but didn't see any other sign of Wang Wei. "What?" Before Rafael could get out anything else, something heavy hit him in the back of the head. He was out before he impacted the snow.

The back of his head pounded, but it was the jouncing that woke Rafael. He felt suspended in a soft cloud, smelling of jerky and fabric softener. Soft light diffused his bed, coming from somewhere above him. A steady thump, thump, thump sound that matched each bump could barely be heard over the howl of the wind. Rafael was warm in his pink coat, but his hat was missing and a cold breeze bit into his exposed ears.

Rafael fought free of the constricting fabric and clawed his way up, towards the light. A hole became visible above him, covered by a flap of fabric. Rafael poked his muzzle through, all that would fit through the small opening. Outside of the protection of what he now recognized as a large dog's backpack, the icy wind stung his nose.

"Help! Help!" Rafael barked and clawed at the cinched hole, which remained stubbornly closed. "Let me out."

The bouncing stopped. "What? Who said that?" a female voice said.

"I'm in your backpack," Rafael yelled as loud as he could.

The backpack swayed and bobbed, and Rafael felt it settle down to the ground. The light dimmed as a shadow fell over the bag, there was a click and then the flap covering the hole flipped open. Rafael stared up into the eyes of a large female husky.

Her muzzle gaped open in surprise, one ear flicking back. She closed her mouth with an audible click and a huff. "You've got to be kidding me. I wondered why my bag felt heavier, but the race was starting and..." She huffed and shook her head. "Now puppy, why are in you my backpack?"

Rafael growled and scratched again at the cinched hole until the husky reached over and opened it. Rafael poked his head out of the bag, but immediately regretted it as the wind whistled through his upturned ears. He pulled his ears flat back against his head, wondering where his hat had gone.

"I'm not a puppy, and I have no idea how I ended up here." Rafael felt around inside his pink coat until he located his wallet. He pulled it out and flipped it open, lifting it out to show the husky his badge. "I'm Detective Rafael Ferreira with the Phoenix Police Department. Hey!"

He yelped as the husky girl reached into the bag with a paw and picked him up by the back of his coat. She lifted him out and then set him gently down on the snow. The sudden movement made Rafael's head swim with a pounding vertigo that sent him reeling. He collapsed face first into the soft powder.

Now that he was outside the backpack Rafael was already starting to shiver. He sat up and looked around himself. He was sitting in a snowbank, surrounded by dark pine trees. Snow was still falling, but the light had waned. He'd been out for hours at least.

The husky held up a paw, hissing in sympathy as she touched the back of his head. Even her feather-light touch made him yelp and jump.

Rafael reached up and probed at the bump on the back of his head. He growled. "Oh, those stupid huskies!"

The husky girl scowled and stood back up to loom over him, crossing her arms across her chest.

"Oh, not you." Rafael could see the hurt in her eyes. He didn't want to piss her off. He had no idea where he was and he couldn't see any other dogs around. "I was talking to three huskies. They hit me in the head...and I guess stuffed me in your pack afterwards."

The husky girl huffed and crossed her arms across her chest. "Three huskies? Leader mostly white with light tan markings?"

Rafael nodded. He was shivering violently now. He didn't dare perk his ears back up for fear of them freezing solid.

The husky girl swore, ears going back flat on her head and baring her teeth. After a few more minutes of swearing she calmed down. She looked around them at the swirling snow and the trees, then pulled a folded map out of the pocket of her coat and began to study it.

Rafael hugged himself, tempted to climb back into the girl's pack. The wind was cutting right through his thin khaki pants. Perfect for a warm Arizona winter and totally inadequate in these subzero temperatures. "What's your name?"

She glanced up at him and grimaced. "Mae, and I'm sorry but it's not been a pleasure to meet you.

Now quiet, I've got to figure out how to get you back to civilization. I think it's closer to go back to the checkpoint at Yentna Station," she stabbed a point on her map and traced with a finger. "Rather than continue on to Skwentna. It will put me behind schedule, but there's no helping it."

"No, you can't take me back!" Rafael protested, jumping up and down in the snow in front of her. "I need to go with you."

"What? Not happening. You're already getting hypothermia." Mae folded back up her map. "Now, get in the bag."

"No." Rafael could tell she wasn't in the mood to talk, but his mission was too important. "Did you see a large golden chow chow with the runners?"

"Yeah, I did. Hard to miss an Asian dog among all the American northern breeds. Why?" Mae crouched down next to him, positioning her bulk between him and the worst of the wind.

"He's one of my confidential informants, here from Arizona for the race." Rafael inched closer to her, grateful for that and the warmth that radiated off her.

"So?"

Rafael almost growled in frustration at the delay this was causing. He'd already lost his chance to catch Wang Wei before the race started, and now he was losing daylight to this cruel prank. "There's a hit out on him. I have to warn him."

Mae snorted. "You're a detective and this Wang Wei is just some criminal that helps you out, right? So why do you care?"

"Wang Wei's information saved the life of me and my partner last month. He warned us of an ambush." Rafael looked away as he was wracked by a particularly violent shiver. "I owe him this much."

"What about the Alaskan authorities, surely they--"

"No!" Rafael growled and met Mae's eyes. "The ambush Wang Wei saved me from... It was other policemen." He gulped. "I don't know who I can trust. I need to warn Wang Wei in person. What little I was able to find out about the assassination is that it's going to happen during the race."

Mae stared at him, her muzzle gaping open for a moment. "That doesn't narrow it down much. The route is over nine hundred miles long!"

"I know. I tried to call him before he left, but he was already on a plane, his phone turned off. I followed him here, hoping to warn him before he left, but there were so many dogs! And then that, that cabron hit me, and well, you know the rest."

Mae growled and narrowed her eyes at him, then sighed heavily. "That cabron is the winner of last year's race, Ingram Yap. Ingram's been trying to bully and intimidate me ever since I came in ahead of him in the qualifiers last month. He probably was trying to slow me down."

She gave a big sigh and held up a paw as Rafael started to speak. "It benefits us both to continue on, so don't worry. I'll take you as far as Skwentna. It's a checkpoint, so all the dogs racing have to check in with the volunteers there."

Rafael brightened and nodded happily. "Thank you!"

He let Mae lift him up and stow him back in the bag. While he bounced along on her back, he dug around in her clothing until he found his hat, which must have fallen off while he was being jostled around. With that back on his head and bundled in her blankets, Rafael almost became warm enough to stop his shivering.

The gentle swaying of the backpack lulling him to sleep competed with the pounding in his head.

Eventually the warmth and the rhythmic motion overcame the nausea and pain and he drifted off to sleep.

A sharp jostle woke Rafael up. Mae barked, the sound muffled by the backpack. The bouncing of the pack increased in pace, slamming him repeatedly into Mae's back. The muted noise made it hard to tell, but the crunching footsteps sounded like they came from more than one pair of feet as the cadence didn't match the frequency of his crashes into Mae.

Rafael burrowed up. The light had faded, and he had to feel around above him for the cinched hole. The cold breeze coming from it guided him and a moment later his gloved paw was free and grasping around blindly, looking for the cinch. Now that he'd seen the outside of the pack he knew how to open it, but the shaking and bumping meant he had to fumble around for several moments before he found it.

The instant he pulled the clasp free and opened the hole, polar air whipped in, instantly freezing his nose and nipping at his eyeballs. Rafael narrowed his eyes and popped his head out. His head pressed against the cloth flap that covered the hole, blocking his view of the sky. The ground rushed by underneath him; the snow swirling in the air glowed with ghostly reflections of Mae's headlamp. Beyond the glare of Mae's LED headlamp the night swallowed the landscape, making it feel like Rafael bounced along in a snow-covered void.

Now that his ears were out of the thick canvas, he could hear two sets of puffing breath and distinguish the thudding of six different feet. A lolling bay sounded out from the night.

"Mae! Mae!" Rafael howled as loud as he could.

"Stay down!" Mae huffed, clearly short of breath. "Moose. Dangerous."

Even from right behind her Rafael could barely make out her words over the howling of the wind. "Moose?" he repeated softly to himself. He'd seen pictures of them, even seen them in person at the zoo in their fenced enclosure. They were massive, sure, and had big horns, but he'd never thought of them as dangerous.

"Raf!" Mae barked. "Flare gun. Bag. Help!"

Rafael dug back into Mae's pack with frantic urgency. He'd remembered feeling a hard plastic edge digging into his side as he'd pulled himself out. He ripped off his gloves and cast about where he thought it had been. His paw brushed something hard, and he grabbed it, pulling it closer. The familiar grip of a pistol was comforting in his grip, despite the strange feeling of the plastic rather than cool iron. Gun in paw, Rafael popped his head back out the hole and pushed aside the top flap.

The bobbing light from Mae's lantern revealed a gigantic moose which towered over Mae and him. The beast's breath huffed out in a plume of steam that froze instantly. Ice crystals hung from the beast's shaggy fur and dripped from its heaving nostrils. The moose lowered its head, centering its wide, flat antlers so that the tips pointed right at Rafael. Each pounding of the giant's hooves sent up clouds of snow and brought the moose closer to Mae.

Rafael looked at the orange, plastic pistol then at the moose's three tons of charging fury. The gun was sized for a bigger dog; Rafael could barely get a finger around the trigger, but compared to the bulk of the moose it looked like a toy.

"Hur...ry!" Mae huffed. It was obvious she couldn't keep this pace up much longer.

Rafael shivered, blinking away the ice crystals that were forming on his eyelashes and lifted the gun, wrapping both paws around it in an effort to keep it steady.

The moose whuffed and sped up, or maybe Mae slowed down, but Rafael knew he had only moments to act. The moose lowered its head still further, but it was so much bigger than them, it put its chin in line with Mae's head. The flap of skin hanging from its neck streamed in the wind. Rafael had never been so terrified. His heart hammered in his chest. He was shaking and not from the cold.

Rafael took a deep breath, sighted down the barrel directly at the white of the moose's eye. The whipping wind and snow obscured his vision, and the backpack was bouncing up and down wildly. Rafael did his best to compensate for the movement, thankful for hours of practice on the range. He willed his shaking paws to still and pulled the trigger.

The flare exploded from the gun with a flash and a pop, streaming towards its target like a comet. The light was so bright in the dark of the night that it burned a red line across his vision.

The light smashed into the moose's nose and burst with a hiss. The moose barked in surprise and slowed down, shaking its head from side to side in an effort to dislodge the burning projectile. Mae continued running, and the beast disappeared into the night behind them.

"I got it, Mae!" Rafael yipped in excitement. "You can stop now."

Mae continued running although she slowed her pace. The bouncing slowed down to a manageable jostle. Perhaps she hadn't heard him.

"The moose stopped chasing us," Rafael cried louder.

"Heard you," Mae huffed. "Not out." She took a deep breath. "Of danger yet."

Now that the adrenaline from the danger with the moose was fading, Rafael was starting to feel cold. As he stared at the darkness and falling snow, he realized what Mae was doing. His flare had done nothing but startle the moose. It might continue to chase them once it recovered. Or there might be more of them.

Rafael wiggled back down into the backpack and felt around until he found the gun's little zipper pouch of ammo. After a lot of fumbling around in the dark, he managed to reload it, just in case.

Mae ran for another few minutes after he finished loading the flare gun, and when she did stop, she first ducked behind a tree. Rafael felt the backpack jostle and a moment later Mae peered down in at him, blinding him with the light of her head lantern.

"Ouch, bright!" Rafael dropped the gun and covered his face with his paws. The LEDs still burned his eyes around his fingers. He blinked tears from his eyes and burrowed his muzzle into the crook of his arm.

"Oops, sorry," Mae said.

Rafael heard a button click, and the light dimmed.

"That better?" Mae asked.

Before Rafael could respond, Mae scooped him out of the bag and squeezed him to her chest in a massive bear hug. Her arms totally engulfed his little body. She was wonderfully warm and soft and Rafael relaxed into her grip, doing his best to hug her back while trapped. He wagged his tail, whipping her arm.

"You did great with that moose. If you hadn't been here, I might have been done for."

"It was nothing," Rafael lied. His heart was still pounding. He'd faced down his share of criminals on the mean streets of downtown Phoenix, but he'd never felt anything near the terror he'd experienced upon seeing that wall of muscled moose barreling down on them.

Mae loosened her grip and lifted him. "You're shivering!"

"Just cold," Rafael said. He wasn't lying, not exactly. The air was so frigid each breath was like a knife to his chest. Where the tip of his muzzle wasn't pressed against Mae, he could feel the cold air almost seeming to go right through him. But being with Mae was like lying down with a furnace.

"Here." She set him carefully back down into the backpack and then fiddled with an outside pocket before passing him a large square plastic gel pack.

"What is it?" Rafael stared at it with fascination. The clear pack was labeled 'Paw warmer' and it was almost as long as his arm.

"It's a chemical gel warmer. Take off the packaging and it will heat up and keep you nice and warm until we get to Skwentna."

Rafael ripped off the printed plastic coating and kneaded the bag inside with his paws. Almost immediately it began to heat up. "Amazing! Heat in a bag."

"Careful not to puncture it with your claws," Mae cautioned him. "Also, it works best if it's close to your fur. Unzip your coat and put it inside." Mae began closing back up the backpack. "Oh and keep that flare gun handy."

"What?" Rafael squeaked.

"Yeah, this area is known as Moose Alley. The forest is dense so the moose like to use the trails. A couple of dogs get chased each year. Guess I'm one of the lucky ones." Mae blew out a breath and gave him a wide mouth smile. "Good thing I had along a stalwart guardian."

Despite himself Rafael felt himself returning Mae's grin. He was still mad at Ingram for pulling this prank and possibly dooming Wang Wei. But it had put him in the right place, at the right time, to protect an innocent dog from harm. Lately so much of his job had become paperwork done behind a desk, and he realized he couldn't remember the last time he'd felt so connected with his job and life. It made him remember why he'd become a cop in the first place.

Despite the cold, Rafael kept his head free of the bag, ready and waiting in case another moose tried to give them a hard time. Ice crystals formed on his whiskers from each breath. He constantly was having to duck his head back into the bag and press his face against the blissfully warm gel-pack, but he persevered.

Other than the crunching of snow under Mae's paws and the shushing of the surrounding pine trees in the wind, the night was silent. He'd grown up in the big city, and night to him meant the pounding thunder of a gunning motorcycle, the conversing of passing dogs, and the rumbling base leaking from a passing car.

Even the sky was unfamiliar. When Rafael craned his head back, he could see hundreds of stars twinkling brightly overhead. The sight awed and humbled him. When he was a puppy, his father had taken him up to the mountains to star gaze, but even there the lights of the city had hidden all but the brightest stars. He began to pick out constellations he'd learned about in grade school. There was Orion, the Hunter. Usually depicted in mythological art as an English Setter. Mae turned a corner and his view shifted, revealing Leo, the roaring lion. Rafael bared his teeth menacingly at the sky.

Rafael ducked back into the bag to warm his ears and nose, and wipe ice crystals from his lashes. When he emerged again, the trees had fallen away. Mae now ran through a wide open field. The light of the stars reflected on the glittering snow, green and purple dancing and flashing like they were running through a gaudy neon nightclub. Rafael's muzzle dropped open. Stars didn't do that. He craned his head around until he looked out over Mae's fluffy ears.

Shimmering hues swung their way through the heavens above them, frolicking and bobbing through the air like a symphony of colors. "Wow..." Rafael chuffed quietly.

Mae chuckled, her ears flickering and Rafael lowered his head. He hadn't realized he'd spoken aloud.

"Quite the sight, eh? I never get tired of it," Mae said over her shoulder. All Rafael could see of her was the back of her head and the tips of her ears, but he could feel her smile.

Rafael looked back up at nature's light show and admitted that he didn't think he ever could either. He opened his muzzle to say as much to Mae, but then shut it again. He didn't want to sound like an uncultured yokel. He stared at the dancing sky without answering for a long minute. "Yeah, it's alright, I guess."

Mae growled. Her ears went back flat against her head and she picked up speed, jostling him around so much he had to grab on lest he bounce right out of the bag. "I know. Alaska's a boring backwater full of hicks, and you can't wait to get back to your big city and palm trees. Yada, yada."

"What? That's not what I meant," Rafael barked out between bounces. But it was too late, the mood had been ruined.

"We're out of Moose Alley and it's still another few hours before we get to the checkpoint, so why don't you get some sleep?" Mae said.

Rafael wanted to apologize to Mae and beg her forgiveness, but he sighed and stayed silent. He'd give her an apology at Skwentna, once she'd had a chance to cool down and when he could do it face to face.

Rafael was woken by another dog barking a greeting to Mae. He uncurled from his ball and popped his nose out of the backpack. The cold crisp air burned his lungs. The air smelled of wet dogs, wood smoke, and dawn. He shivered and pulled his head back in.

He unzipped his coat and pressed the gel pack to his muzzle until he was warmed up, then tucked the pack back against his chest.

"Where am I in the standings?" He overheard Mae say.

"Not too bad," an unfamiliar dog replied. "You're the eighth dog to check in from your time group. Won't know your overall standing until I radio in your time."

"You going to press on?" the other dog asked Mae.

"Not yet. I need a few hours of sleep before I continue," Mae said and began taking off the backpack. Rafael ducked back out of sight, suddenly conscious of being seen. He didn't want his presence here to get Mae in trouble, or to be forcibly sent back to Anchorage before he could save Wang Wei.

The backpack hit the ground with a thump and then he heard Mae fumbling with the opening. She reached in a paw and grabbed him by the back of his pink coat, pulling him out. Rafael struggled against her grip as the cold air hit him.

"Don't worry, no one's watching," Mae whispered to him as she sat him down.

Rafael shook himself and then straightened his hat and coat. His boots crunched on the snow as he spun about. They were in an open field covered in an icy layer of snow. The sun was barely peeking over the horizon in the distance, the light glittering and bright on the almost untouched expanse of snow. A trail snaked away into the distance, disappearing into the trees near the horizon.

Two snowmobiles were lined up next to the poles of a suspended banner. It read Welcome in big red letters. Underneath in smaller black print was Skwentna Checkpoint. A few dogs congregated next to the far pole holding up the banner. A large fluffy Saint Bernard dog wore a red jacket with a white cross on the back, first aid for the runners. The rest of the crowd were huskies and malamutes. A few wore backpacks and Rafael judged them to be other runners taking a break at the checkpoint.

A white, curly-tailed American Eskimo holding a clipboard was walking away from him and Mae, headed towards the knot of dogs. The back of her jacket read volunteer in big yellow letters.

"I'd talk to Kiska about your Chow," Mae said, bobbing her head towards the retreating American Eskimo. "She's one of the race coordinators. If Wang Wei has come through here already, she'll know."

"And if he hasn't?" Rafael shivered and tucked his tail between his legs. He'd only been out of Mae's backpack for a few minutes and he was already getting cold.

"Then it means we beat him here." Mae held out a paw. "And then all you'll have to do is hang out here until he comes through, tell him your piece, and then hitch a ride back with Kiska."

"Oh." Rafael dug the toe of his boot into the snow and ducked his head. "I'm sorry about last night. I..." Rafael took a deep breath. He had begun to like Mae and the fact that she was mad at him had left a hard knot of dread in his stomach. "I wanted to sound more traveled than I am, in order to impress you. To tell the truth, I've lived in Phoenix my entire life. This is the first time I've ever left Arizona. I'm terrified, and cold, but it didn't excuse what I said last night. I'm sorry."

Without warning Mae dropped down next to him. Her muzzle gaped open and her tail wagged furiously. "I accept your apology." She pressed her nose up against his for a moment then stood back up, brushing snow off her pants. "You look cold. Hurry and go talk to Kiska and by the time you get back I should have my tent set up."

"Thanks," Rafael said, then took off after the white dog.

Her long strides meant that she'd reached the gathering of dogs by the time he was able to catch up to her. She was already in conversation with them when Rafael came up behind her.

"Excuse me, Kiska?" he barked politely to get her attention.

Every dog in the huddle turned to stare down at him, and as one their muzzles dropped open in surprise and one ear each cocked back. One of the huskies burst into riotous laughter and Rafael belatedly recognized him as the dog that had tricked him back at the starting line. Ingram. Rafael pointedly ignored him and addressed Kiska.

"I'm looking for this dog. His name is Wang Wei. He's a golden Chow." Rafael fumbled with the zipper on his pocket for a moment, the unfamiliar gloves and cold making his normally dexterous paws clumsy. Finally he prevailed and held up Wang Wei's photo, doing his best to straighten it out. His trip in Mae's backpack had left it rumpled and creased.

Kiska gaped at him, barely glancing at the picture. "What kind of dog are you? Are you a dog? And how did you get all the way out here?"

"Hitched a ride," Rafael responded. "And I'm a Chihuahua." When everyone stared at him blankly he continued. "From Arizona."

"Oh, my. You're a long way from home." Kiska tutted.

"Yes, and the faster I find this dog, the sooner I can get back to my nice, warm home." Rafael raised the picture higher, holding it in front of his face.

Around them the group of dogs broke apart, the huskies and malamutes gathered up their backpacks. The medical Saint Bernard wandered off to greet two new dogs arriving at the checkpoint.

"You just missed him. He got here about an hour ago. Just before the sun came up. Stuck around long enough to check in, then took off again," Kiska said.

Rafael cursed and stuffed Wang Wei's photo back into his pocket. "Thanks." He turned to go.

"Popular guy, that Chow," Kiska mused.

"What do you mean?" Rafael said, his hackles stiffening. He'd known assassins were after Wang Wei, but his whole plan hinged on beating them to their target and warning him of the danger.

"You're the second dog this morning to ask after him." Kiska shrugged. "Anyway, if you came by air you're out of luck. No airstrip at the Finger Lake checkpoint."

"I didn't. Um, can I ask who else asked you about him?" Rafael shivered violently. His gel pack was failing, turning to a cooling lump in his coat and the cold began to creep down through his hat and gloves.

"It was," Kiska turned and pointed to a group of distant figures jogging along the trail. Even as they watched, they disappeared into the trees beyond the meadow. "Oh, they left without saying goodbye. Anyway, one of that group."

Rafael growled and stomped his feet in an attempt to warm up. "Which one, specifically?"

"They all arrived in a clump, and it was a bit of chaos, let me tell you." Kiska cocked her head, her ears flicking as she thought. "One of the huskies, I'm sure of it. Was it Bernie? No. Oh, yes, it was Ingram! Such a nice dog. He wanted to check on Wang Wei because it is his first race. Ingram and his pack are seasoned runners, you see. They told me they like to check up on first timers."

"Oh, that's nice of them," Rafael said, but inside he was tensing up. Nothing that Mae had said about Ingram pointed towards him being a good dog.

"Yes, it is." Kiska leaned down and cocked her head. "I need to go check in these runners, but you should go see the medic and make sure you don't have frost-bite. You're not dressed properly for this weather."

Rafael shivered harder and nodded.

Kiska bobbed her head in satisfaction and bounded off to greet the new dogs, who were now engaged in animated conversation with the medic. Rafael turned and shuffled back to where he'd left Mae. As promised, a colorful one-dog tent was set up and Mae's curly tail was just disappearing through the zippered opening. Rafael followed her inside.

Already inside the tent was significantly warmer than outside. Rafael hadn't realized just how much the slight breeze had been chilling him until he was out of it. His shivering subsided some. The tent was small, and Mae's fluffy husky body took up most of the space. If Rafael had been any bigger, he wouldn't have fit. Being this close to Mae he could feel the heat radiating from her, and the scent of her made his tail wag involuntarily.

"Good news?" Mae asked him as she shook out a body-bag style sleeping bag that had been tied to the bottom of her pack.

Rafael shook his head. "No, bad news and worse. Wang Wei has come and gone already."

Mae unzipped the side of her bag in one smooth motion. "So, I suppose next you're going to ask me to take you with me to the next checkpoint."

Rafael shook his head. "No. Kiska and the medic both have snowmobiles. I'm sure if I explain to them the need they'll give me a lift. I just came back to say goodbye and to ask you a question."

"Oh." Mae blinked at him and he would have sworn she looked almost disappointed, but no, he had to be wrong.

"So what's your question?" Mae said, wriggling out of her coat. The fur underneath was snow white and looked pleasantly soft. Rafael caught himself wondering what it'd be like to cuddle up to that fur. He cut that thought off and pushed it away.

"If I told you that Ingram was checking up on a first time runner, to give advice to a less experienced dog, what would you say?"

"I'd say you must have hit your head on something." Mae flashed him a grin. "Ingram is ruthlessly competitive. He'd never willingly do anything to help a new racer. Why?"

"That's what I was afraid of." Rafael grimaced and relayed what had happened. "I'm afraid Ingram and his buddies might be the assassins after Wang Wei."

Mae opened her muzzle to argue with him, then shut it again. Her face and ears flickered through a variety of emotions, obviously thinking through Rafael's accusation. Finally she shook herself as if shaking off water.

"No, I don't think so. I think he was probably just upset that a first-time racer, and a foreign breed dog at that, beat him to the checkpoint." Mae sighed and plopped down on her sleeping bag, looking longingly at her pillow for a long moment before turning her attention back to Rafael. "However, I wouldn't put it past him. Give me a few minutes to pack back up and we'll head out."

"Mae, I appreciate the help you've given me so far, but get some sleep. The snowmobiles--"

"Aren't allowed on the trail the runners use. They have to stay on the roads," Mae said, cutting him off. "You wouldn't be able to meet up with Wang Wei until the Finger Lake Checkpoint, at the soonest, and Ingram could catch him long before then."

"How, if Wang Wei's the faster runner?"

"Fast isn't everything in the Iditarod," Mae said. "It's about endurance."

While Mae packed back up her tent, Rafael went back to talk to Kiska. By the time he was done explaining to her what he needed, Mae had finished packing her bag. She jogged over to them, her pack slung over one shoulder.

"I'm ready to go," Rafael told her, while marveling at how fast she'd packed her backpack and how small of a bundle her tent was once she'd taken it down and rolled it up.

Mae put the bag on the ground and Rafael crawled inside.

As they left Rafael heard Kiska call out to them, "Mae, good luck!"

"What was that about?" Mae huffed out as she jogged away.

"I took some of your advice," Rafael said, snuggling down into her spare clothes. He stayed there until he was warm again, then as much as he could he kept his head outside the bag to watch the scenery go by.

He'd never thought of snow as beautiful before. Pictures he'd seen of snowy landscapes had seemed to him bleak and almost monochromatic. However, as he gazed about it was the first word that popped into his mind.

Snow draped the trees in coats of white. Flashes of blue and green pine-tree needles poked from beneath the snow. In the distance snow-capped mountains dominated the distant horizon. A rabbit startled by Mae's steps on the snow broke out of the bushes and hopped along in front of them for several moments before veering off back into the underbrush. The sun never rose much above the horizon, which gave the sky a perpetual pink blush of dawn. The sun glittered on the undisturbed snow and lit the surrounding trail in an ever changing patchwork.

"This is part of the Northern Lights trail," Mae said to him during one of her running breaks. "It's one of my favorites."

"I can see why," Rafael replied with a genuine smile.

After several hours Rafael twisted around in the pack so he could talk to Mae easier as well as to help watch the trail ahead of them. They had a pleasant conversation, and Mae told him all about growing up in the backwoods of Alaska and the fight she'd had when she'd announced her desire to be a runner like her father.

"What was the big deal?" Rafael asked.

"It wasn't--" she huffed, and sped up. "--feminine. They lamented that I'd never find a mate and get puppies of my own, since I spent all my spare time running."

Rafael grimaced. "I'm sorry," he said, and meant it. "I understand how hard it can be when it feels like everyone is arranged against you."

"Because of your size?"

"There are other Chihuahuas on the force." Rafael sighed. "But yes, we have to do more to prove ourselves than the bigger dogs. When I was promoted to detective over a lot of larger dogs that had been there longer, a few of my co-workers, well, I think I already said enough about that." Rafael fell silent.

The only sounds were Mae's harsh breathing and the crunch of her boots on the snow. Somewhere in the distance a hawk cried.

"I feel like, if I can save my informant, and get this big bust, I'll prove them wrong," Rafael said finally.

One of Mae's paws reached back over her shoulder. Rafael grasped it, sharing a moment of solidarity. Rafael leaned forward, over Mae's shoulder, and licked Mae's cheek. He knew hs blushing would have been visible through his short fur and was glad Mae couldn't see him.

"Mae, I--" Rafael began as he slid back into place, but Mae cut him off.

"There, up ahead!" Her paw pulled away, leaving him off balance. "That's Ingram, I'm sure of it."

Rafael leaned to the side to see around the back of Mae's head. Far in the distance stood a group of dogs. They were off the main trail, almost at the tree line. Rafael could just make out the marks they'd made where they'd cut off the trail. Three white and gray furred figures were chasing, herding really, a fourth gold furred dog into the woods.

"His coat," Mae said in response to his unasked question. "Ingram has been doing the race for years and has corporate sponsors. I recognize the placement and colors of the patches."

Mae sped up, her lope turning into a jog, and then a sprint. Rafael thought Mae had been pushing the pace before, and now he found out how wrong he'd been. Snow flew from her boots. Rafael jounced around so much he had to throw his arms around Mae's neck or risk flying from the pack.

As they reached the point where the dog's tracks left the path, Mae slowed down. The other dogs had forded a path through the snow, and Mae took advantage of the work they'd done by placing her feet in their paw-prints.

One thing that struck Rafael in Alaska was how still and silent it was. Because of that, when there was a sound it seemed louder than it should have been and it carried. Between the crunches of Mae's boots on the snow came a dull thwack. It took Rafael a moment to register the sounds as fists connecting with flesh.

Rafael drew in a hissing breath. "Hurry," he whispered as they neared the trees.

Mae ducked under a low-hanging branch sending a small flurry of snow spraying down on Rafael's head. He brushed it off while Mae stopped and knelt down to pull off her backpack. The area underneath the trees was relatively clear of snow and Rafael emerged from the pack onto a soft bed of fallen pine needles. He was carrying Mae's flare gun gripped in both paws.

Mae left her pack and jogged off into the trees. Rafael did his best to keep up with his short legs. He didn't dare lose Mae in this forest. The way sound echoed was eerie, and he wasn't sure he'd be able to find Mae if he lost her, even if she was calling to him.

Despite the fact that she was at least three times larger than him, Mae passed with barely a sound, like a ghost. Rafael felt like an elephant blundering along behind her. He must have stepped on every twig, branch, pine-cone, and crunchy leaf between him and their goal.

Thankfully it seemed Ingram and his pack were too involved in what they were doing to Wang Wei to notice. Mae stopped, held up a paw and pointed. Rafael stepped up next to her and peered through the underbrush. Ingram and his pack had Wang Wei surrounded and were pounding on him. Wang Wei had curled into a ball, his front paws over his face. Blood streaked Wang Wei's golden coat, and he whimpered in pain as the other dogs hit. As they watched Ingram picked up a tire iron which Rafael hadn't noticed previously lying by his feet. Ingram lifted it above his head, ready to strike.

Rafael took a big breath, lifted the flare gun, and then stepped forward shouting, "Stop, police!"

Ingram's head snapped up and everyone stopped moving. In the sudden silence, the pop and hiss of the flare-gun going off was deafeningly loud. The flare shot up from Rafael's outstretched paws to burst above the trees in a flash of red.

Ingram whirled to face Rafael, snarling, the tire iron still held above his head. Before Rafael could react Ingram charged towards him. His two pack buddies turned to face him, leaving off their attack on Wang Wei, but otherwise made no move to help.

"I said stop!" Rafael dropped the now empty gun and scrambled back.

Ingram swung at him. Rafael darted to the side and dropped to all fours. The tire iron whistled overhead, missing Rafael's head by mere inches. He felt it brush the tip of his pointy ears and realized that at some point he must have lost his hat. Again.

Mae snarled and jumped over Rafael's head. She wrapped a paw around Ingram's arm, and with her other one began trying to wrestle the tire iron out of his grip.

"Mae, what're you doing?" Ingram growled at her.

"Stopping you from making a big mistake, Ingram," Mae growled back.

Rafael was trapped underneath, darting this way and that between the bigger dogs while trying to avoid being stepped on.

From his left came a yelp of pain and a deep growl. Rafael took a chance and glanced that direction to see that Wang Wei had risen and taking advantage of his tormentors' distraction, pounced on them from behind. Despite the fact that he was injured and outnumbered, it looked like Wang Wei had Ingram's pack mates taken care of.

He was so engrossed in watching Wang Wei thrash the two huskies that he lost track of feet. A boot stomped down and caught the tip of his tail. Rafael yelped and reacted on instinct, twisting around and sinking his teeth into the owner's leg. Only after did he think to check who he'd bitten. He tried to glance up, but all he could see were parkas and pants. Instead he inhaled deeply. The scent was similar to Mae's, but not her. He ground his mouth down harder, biting deeply into Ingram's leg. He tasted blood.

Ingram lifted his leg, prepared to stomp. The move jerked Rafael's head and pulled him up. He clawed at Ingram's boot with his front paws, trying to pull his lower body up. Ingram stomped into the snow.

The boot came down hard on Rafael's left leg and tail, and he had to grit his teeth to keep from crying out and releasing Ingram. His leg throbbed; he couldn't tell if it was broken or not, but the pain was incredible. His vision wavered as Ingram lifted his foot. Rafael's flailing front paws connected with Ingram's leg.

He dug in his claws, clinging tight, opened his jaw, and pulled himself up Ingram's calf. He waited until Ingram stomped down again, catching nothing but snow and pine needles, then bit down as hard as he could right at the back bend of Ingram's knee.

The big dog howled and Rafael's worldview turned into a falling jumble of fur, snow, and leaf litter. Next thing he knew he was buried under a pile of fur and suffocating under Ingram's bulk. By the time he crawled free Mae had Ingram on his stomach, her knee in his back and one arm around his neck. Wang Wei had Ingram's two pals, one massive paw holding each of them face-first against the ground.

Mae yipped with excitement when she saw him. "Are you alright?"

Rafael rolled over and gently prodded his leg. He winced in pain. Almost certainly broken. "I'm alive," he said, flopping over to his back and panting. "We saved Wang Wei, that's what counts."

"Detective Ferreira!" Wang Wei barked. Only Rafael's long acquaintance with the big dog allowed him to hear the relief and thanks in Wang Wei's voice. "To say I'm shocked to see you would be an understatement."

Rafael turned his head and gave Wang Wei a tired smile. "Hah. By the way, your life is in danger."

In response Wang Wei let out a rumbling basso laugh that shook snow from the trees above them.

Mae frowned at Wang Wei then turned her gaze back to Rafael. "Raffie, I thought you were a better shot with a gun than that. What happened back there?"

Rafael wrinkled his nose. He hated being called by a nickname, but then again he owed Mae a huge debt of gratitude. So instead he just replied. "I didn't miss."

She shook her head and turned her attention back to Ingram lying prone under her. "And you, Ingram! What were you thinking?"

"I was thinking I was broke and needed the money," Ingram growled back as he struggled against her.

The roar of snowmobiles drowned out the rest of Ingram's reply. Probably for the best.

Rafael smiled widely and shouted, "Cavalry is here."

After what felt like hours to Rafael and his throbbing leg, but was probably more like fifteen minutes, Kiska, riding double with the medical Saint Bernard from Skwentna station, roared up along with a string of local police dogs.

It took Rafael quite a while to explain what had happened and why he was here. But eventually, after repeatedly showing them his badge and they'd made a call in to his supervisor in Arizona --- that made Rafael wince but there was no help for it --- the local police agreed to arrest Ingram and his pack members on charges of attempted murder.

Rafael's story was confirmed again when they searched the dogs and found an unregistered .22 in Ingram's pocket along with Wang Wei's picture, on the back of which was written *Introduce him to the man in black* in big, block letters.

The medic splinted Rafael's leg and loaded him onto a stretcher attached to the back of one of the snowmobiles, layering him in blankets.

Mae came up as they were strapping him down. She leaned over him and gave him a long hug, then pulled away and planted a kiss on him, muzzle to muzzle. It was hard to wag his tail, buried as it was, but Rafael tried. Mae was brave, determined, and beautiful. This morning he'd have said he'd never have a shot at a girl like her, yet here she was.

Rafael returned the kiss with gusto. Mae was a fantastic kisser, sensuous, slow, and teasing. When she pulled away she did so slowly, giving the tip of his nose a lick as she did. She stood and stepped away as the snowmobile roared to life. Rafael twisted to watch her face as they pulled away.

"Mae!" he yelled over the rumble of the engine.

She waved and blew him a kiss.

Rafael was kept in the hospital overnight for observation. They said along with his broken leg he was suffering from mild hypothermia and dehydration.

His broken leg lay on the bed entombed in a thick cast. They'd wrapped him in warm blankets and made him drink what felt like gallons of hot tea.

Over the nurses protestations that he needed sleep, Rafael made them turn on the television to show news of the race. A lot of the coverage was about the surprise arrest of race darling Ingram Yap, charged with the attempted murder of another racer. They praised the quick thinking of an out-of-town detective with saving the victim's life, but gave no mention of Mae's assistance. Rafael flipped the television off in irritation.

Early the next morning the call he'd been expecting came. Rafael gulped, steeled himself, and took the portable hand-set from the nurse.

"Good morning, Captain," Rafael said with false cheer. He was helped along by the drugs for the pain, which buoyed him in a cloud of hazy euphoria.

"Lieutenant Ferreira, good work up there," the Captain replied.

Rafael pulled the phone away from his ear and stared at it for a moment before putting it back. "Excuse me?" He'd been sure he'd lost his job. After all, he'd gone haring off to Alaska, out of his jurisdiction without permission or backup, and he'd dragged civilians into the mess to boot.

"Captain, I'm just a detective, not a --"

The Captain cut him off with a woof. "As of now you are. You just made Lieutenant and earned yourself a nice bonus to go with it. Thanks to you, Wang Wei has agreed to turn state's witness. Last night we arrested dogs we've been after for years, but never been able to get charges to stick. Well, they won't be able to weasel out of this one."

"Wang Wei, is he alright? I lost track of him when the medics took me away."

"He's fine. A little bruised up, but fine. He's in protective custody now. Guarded round the clock by a team of our finest."

"Thank the lord." Rafael blew out a breath in relief.

"Indeed." There was a muffled sound; then the Captain returned to the line. "They tell me you'll be out of the hospital by this afternoon. I'll arrange your return flights and have someone pick you up at the airport in Phoenix."

Rafael licked his chops. Last night he'd been making plans for what to do when he was fired. Now he was looking at a promotion and a raise, along with a big bonus and status as hero of the department. He thought of Mae and their journey of the last two days.

"Sir, that's not necessary." He took a deep breath, realizing his paws were shaking. He tightened his grip on the phone. "I quit."

Dead silence came through the other end of the line.

"I quit," Rafael repeated with finality. A weight lifted from his shoulders, a burden he hadn't realized he'd been carrying until it was gone. "I'm staying in Alaska." He hung up the phone before his boss could say anything else.

Rafael spent the rest of the morning on the phone ordering plane tickets, hotel rooms, and finally calling movers to pack up his apartment in Phoenix. When the doctors gave him the all clear that afternoon he hopped in a cab to his first destination, awkwardly navigating the snow with his crutches.

By the end of the week he was getting around on the crutches like a pro and easily descended the stairs off the plane in Nome with little problem. Despite the snow and blowing wind he was pleasantly warm in his new weather-appropriate outdoor gear.

He'd spent the week eagerly following the runner's progress in the news, easy to do as he'd discovered that the race seemed to be playing on every television in the state of Alaska. He wasn't sure exactly when Mae was set to finish, but the predictions had her coming in later that day.

Rafael hobbled over to join the crowd around the Burled Arch, a great wooden thing that marked the official end of the race. The snow around the wooden arch was packed down from so many boots on it. The winner along with five others had come in yesterday, and from what he'd seen on the news, hundreds of dogs had come out to cheer.

The crowd today was much smaller, about two dozen dogs all told, bundled up against the cold. Some held banners for various racers. Rafael left his rolled up in his backpack for now. Once he got it out, he'd be unable to use his crutches.

A cry went up from those closer to the arch. Rafael leaned forward and squinted. A figure appeared in the distance, a speck against the snow. Rafael would recognize that form anywhere. He planted his crutches and pulled his banner out of the side pocket of his bag.

It seemed to take ages. The running dot grew steadily larger, eventually resolving into Mae's lithe form. Her tongue hung out as she panted, her breath steaming in the cold air. She looked thinner than she had when last Rafael saw her, her eyes sunken in fatigue, but a large grin split her muzzle and her eyes sparkled with joy.

Rafael unfurled the vinyl banner. He lifted it by the sticks at either end and spread it out high above his head. Of course, high above Rafael's head meant chest height to the rest of the crowd, but he was confident Mae would see it. Mae the Champion was printed on it in bright red text.

Mae sprinted the last hundred yards to the arch, and the crowd roared as she passed underneath. Rafael barked Mae's name along with them, so excited he wanted to jump up and down. Instead he settled for waving the banner about above his head and wagging his tail at supersonic speed.

"Rafael!" Mae whooped. She ran right past the race officials who had come up to greet her and scooped Rafael up into a tight hug. Rafael's crutches and his banner went clattering down onto the snow, but he didn't care. He hugged Mae back fiercely. The crowd tittered. Rafael ignored them.

After a moment Mae set him down. Rafael balanced precariously on one leg, doing his best not to put weight on his cast while Mae retrieved his crutches with a sheepish open-mouthed grin. Once he was steady again he slung off his backpack and rooted around inside until he found the gift he'd gotten for her.

Mae crouched down next to him, her head tilted curiously.

"For you." He pulled out the statue and presented it with a little flourish.

Mae laughed and covered her muzzle with her paws, eyes shining with mirth as she looked down at the little ceramic cactus decorated with sparkly snow. She plucked it from him and pecked him on the cheek. "It's perfect."

"Congratulations on the big finish. Seventh place!" Rafael grinned and tried to hide his blush, but he knew his ears betrayed him.

"Thank you. I'm surprised to see you here. I thought you'd rush back to warm Arizona as soon as you got the chance." Mae's tail wagged.

Her scent filled his nose, she smelled of ice, pine trees, and dirt. He'd never smelled anything more delightful. Snow swirled around them, the chill breeze ruffling Rafael's ears. His breath came out in little puffs and he blinked icicles from his lashes.

Rafael reached over and placed a paw in hers, next to the cactus statue. "Why would I want to leave paradise?"

Suddenly, Chihuahua

This story was originally published in *What the Fox?!* edited by Fred Patten and released by Thurston Howl Publications in April 2018.

The dog came tearing out of a cat flap set into the front door and was gnawing on my ankle before I'd barely registered its presence. He was the ugliest thing I've ever seen. The tan Chihuahua had an under-bite, so that his lower teeth stuck out beyond his lip, making him look like a bulldog, his nose was slightly off center and one eye was milky white. On top of that, his head was comically larger than his spindly body.

I leaned over and grabbed the tiny thing by the back of the neck, trying to pull it away. It growled low in its throat and didn't let go. I tugged harder and my pants gave way with a sharp ripping sound.

Unfamiliar routes were my bane. If I'd known this house had a crazy Chihuahua I would have been on guard sooner. I'd seen the flap in the door, but based on the size had thought it was for cats.

"Nugget! Chicken Nugget! You bad dog," a feminine voice scolded. A woman, probably in her early twenties, came out of the front door of the house the little monster had come from.

I lifted Nugget and held him out towards the woman. A scrap of blue fabric from my pants hung from the Chihuahua's mismatched teeth.

"Oh, thank you," the woman said as she took him from me. "I'm so sorry about that. He is such a terror. I thought for sure I'd locked the flap, but somehow this little devil always manages to get out anyway." She shook her head and glared at the little dog. There was some warmth in her look, but underneath it was glimmer of real exasperation.

Anger welled up in me over my ruined pants. But my supervisor had been clear that one more outburst at a postal 'customer' and I would be fired, so I gritted my teeth and did my best to keep my voice even as I replied, "I'm fine, thanks."

The woman shrugged at me, clearly dismissing my presence, before disappearing back into the house.

Back in my mail truck after completing my circuit, I pulled up my leg to examine the damage to my slacks. A big chunk had been torn off all the way up the calf.

Even worse, Nugget's bite had caught my skin. Blood had soaked into the cuff of my white sock, but I didn't bother to pull out the first aid kit since it had already scabbed over.

A fresh surge of anger ran through me and I pounded on the steering wheel hard enough to bruise my palms. A new pair of pants was not in the budget for this month, or any month really.

I made it home without further incident, but the wound on my ankle itched furiously as I began slicing the veggies and frying the steak strips for fajitas.

At five-thirty, exactly, the front door banged open.

"Dinner's almost ready," I yelled. If I left the stove now my shells would burn.

"Not staying, darling," Kirby, my husband, called from the front room. "Bowling league tonight."

"But--" I started to protest.

"No time to chat." He stepped into the kitchen, pecked me on the cheek, and then was gone, the front door slamming closed behind him.

I stood, frozen in the act of flipping a fajita shell until the heat burned thumb. I yelped and jumped away.

The clock was edging up towards six, so where were my kids? I dug through my purse for my cell phone.

"Where r u?" I typed, eyes narrowing to glare at my daughter's picture on the screen, as if I could send my glare through the phone along with the words. "Dinner getting cold."

"At Brianna's," came the terse reply from my oldest, Maria. "Studying for a test tomorrow. Home late. Had pizza. Love you."

Taya, my youngest, replied a few minutes later. "On way home now. Already ate at Staci's house."

The mounds of food I'd spent the last hour preparing stared back at me from the table. I growled and got the Tupperware, slamming the cupboards closed.

My hands shook with anger as I began scooping the food into the plastic containers. The shaking grew worse and my trembling fingers dropped the serving spoon. It fell into a container I'd already filled, tipping it over and dumping fajita mix off the table and all over the floor.

"¡Qué putada!" I screamed, frustrated, hungry, and exhausted. One more thing to clean up.

I moved to get a rag, but my whole body began to shake hard enough to make my teeth chatter as if I was freezing.

Without warning the whole kitchen seemed to expand around me; the walls becoming farther apart, the table and then the chair bottoms rising above my head.

A moment later soft navy fabric fell over my entire body, blocking my vision. I struggled out of the mound of clothes with difficulty. My fingers didn't seem to be working properly and I couldn't get a grip on the fabric to lift it. I thrashed my way free and tried to stand, but my legs were shaky. What was going on?

I fell to all fours, a strangely comfortable position, and glanced around. The colors of the kitchen washed out, reds becoming pale brown and yellow and the navy of my uniform faded to pale blue. My whole body tingled oddly. I twisted my head to look down at myself, trying to figure out what was wrong.

Soft brown fur came into view, along with a thin tail that curled above my back. The tail wagged back and forth and I realized that I could feel it there on my butt.

Suddenly, somehow, I'd become a Chihuahua.

After a few moments of balancing on my spindly back legs and craning my neck I spotted where I'd left my cell phone on the kitchen counter, next to my purse.

I backed up and charged. My claws scrabbled for purchase on the linoleum, but I managed to build up some speed even in the tiny kitchen. I jumped as hard and high as I could, only to smack headfirst into the drawers, not even halfway up.

I stumbled around dazed. Above me, my phone chimed and buzzed with an incoming text message, the vibration moving the phone until a corner peaked out over the edge. The phone might as well have been on the moon for all the good it did me down on the floor.

The front door creaked and a girl's voice called.

"Mom, I'm home!"

"Thank heaven!" I trotted out into the living room. "Taya, you have to help me."

Taya blinked down at me in surprise and shut the door behind her, shedding her muddy tennis shoes and backpack onto the floor.

"Young lady, you know better than that. Put your shoes on the porch and pick up your backpack," I snapped at her, stomping one little Chihuahua foot.

"Mom, are you home?" Taya said as if I hadn't spoken. She peered around in bewilderment. "Where are you? And when did we get a dog?"

"What?" My whole body began shaking again. "I'm right in front of you!"

"Man, this thing barks a lot," Taya muttered to herself.

"I'm not barking, I'm talking!" I jumped around at her legs, but it was no use. From her comment it was obvious all my daughter heard when I spoke was the barking of an excited dog.

Taya walked into the kitchen, groaned at the mess, and began to clean up. "Dad's gonna be pissed."

One by one my family got home, each commenting on my absence, the pile of clothes in the kitchen, and speculating on the strange dog. I continued to yell pleas for help, but like Taya, they heard only barks.

Finally they went to bed, shutting me into a bathroom alone. I curled up on the rug and whined myself to sleep.

I woke up the next morning stiff, sore, and naked, but thankfully human again. The hardwood floor was cold on my bare feet as I tip-toed my way into the bedroom, put on pajamas, and slipped into bed.

Kirby rolled over as I tugged the covers up, throwing his arm around me. A few moments later he yawned and opened his eyes. "Juana? Where've you been?" he mumbled sleepily.

"Friend emergency. Thanks for watching her dog for me while I was out." I'd had a lot of time to think up an excuse while locked in the bathroom overnight.

"Without your purse? Or pho--"

My alarm buzzed, cutting him off. I slapped it off, pecked him on the cheek, and rolled out of bed, rushing into the bathroom to forestall further questions. By the time I got out he was fast asleep again.

After picking up my truck full of mail, I parked in the same place as yesterday and began delivering letters.

"Hey, hey! Go away! My house!" A low voice growled.

I stopped, startled, as I hadn't seen anyone around. A big black lab growled at me from behind a chain link fence.

The black lab opened its mouth. "Stop! Don't come any closer, you intruder!" the dog barked.

I froze, startled, and stared at the dog. "What? Did you just speak to me?"

"Yes I did!" the dog barked. "I told you to stay away from my yard, you stranger."

"I won't go into your yard, I promise." My face heated with embarrassment.

"See that you don't." The dog sniffed and sat, watching me warily through the fence as I passed.

I stopped again with my hand reaching for the mailbox and looked at the dog. Feeling a bit silly I said, "don't be startled. I'm just going to deliver these letters and be on my way."

The black lab huffed and didn't reply. I took that as assent, popping the letters into the box before speed walking away.

Had that dog really *talked* to me? Was I going crazy? I pulled out my cell phone.

"About yesterday." I texted to Taya. I sent the text, but then hesitated. Taya had been the one to get home and find me, but I had no idea how to word my question without sounding crazy. While I was thinking I dropped mail off at the next house. My phone pinged before I figured it out.

"NP. Dad explained. RU ok?" Taya texted back.

"Fine. Everything is fine now."

"Gr8. Wish we could keep the dog. So cute." Taya followed up with a slew of emoticon hearts and kisses, then another ping. "What's the dog's name?"

How to respond to that? I chewed on my lip, staring at the phone. What if this happened again?

"Bella," I texted back with a smile. If I was to be a dog, I might as well constantly be told I was pretty. "We'll be dog sitting her in the future, whenever my friend needs us to." I tucked the phone away.

"Hey, you! Stay away! This is my dead squirrel," a dog barked at me from behind a white picket fence.

"I don't want your dead squirrel," I answered absently, focused as I was on my bag and gathering the mail for the next house.

A man walking towards me on the sidewalk stopped and gawked. "Lady, what is your problem?" he yelled, crossing the street to avoid me.

Nugget's house was coming up next. He was a Chihuahua and I'd turned into a one yesterday after he'd bit me; I hoped he was home, so I could ask him about it. The connection was tenuous, but it was the only explanation I could come up with.

I took a deep breath to steady my pounding heart, opened the gate, and started up the walk. Their mailbox was mounted on the wall next to the front door and yesterday Nugget had come after me only after I'd turned my back.

The pet flap squeaked. I turned and crouched, catching Nugget by his collar just as he lunged for my ankle, again.

"Got ya," I crowed, lifting the little dog.

Nugget blinked at me in surprise, and then barked in a high pitched voice while squirming wildly. "Put me down so I can kill you properly, invader."

"Not until you've answered a few questions." The collar dug into his throat, so I shifted my grip to encompass the scruff of skin on the back of his neck.

"Intruder!" Nugget screamed, continuing to squirm and snap.

The same woman came out the door, giving Nugget an exasperated glare. "Thank you for catching him. He's such a handful!" She held out her hands.

"Just a sec." I pulled the thrashing Nugget close, struggling to keep hold of him and the heavy bag of mail. "What did you do to me yesterday?"

"The bite was a warning to never come back!" Nugget was almost foaming at the mouth now he was so frantically barking and flailing. "Obviously, stupid human."

"Tell me how to break the curse," I hissed, anger making my voice tight. A tingling tightness ran over my skin and I could feel myself beginning to shake.

"Curse? I don't know what you are talking about! Get out of my territory." Nugget twisted free, leaping for the ground, but the woman from the house caught him before he landed.

"Bad Chicken Nugget," she scolded, sweeping away into the house, not even giving me a backward glance.

I staggered away, trembling so violently I could barely work the catch on the gate. It finally popped open and I lurched onto the sidewalk.

My bag of mail felt as if someone was filling it full of rocks, getting heavier and heavier with each step. My vision narrowed to a strip, the colors fading and dulling. I managed two steps more and collapsed into the bushes.

When I thrashed free of my clothing I found myself once again a dog. I lifted my muzzle and screamed at the sky in frustration.

Once I calmed down a bit I sat in the dirt and tried to figure out what to do. My mail truck was parked just one block over, but there was no way I would be able to get the door open. It wasn't just the problem of my paws not being able to manipulate things, but as a Chihuahua I was just too short. Plus, I didn't dare leave my bag and clothes just sitting here under a bush, for anyone to steal. Thinking about my clothes made me remember my pockets, and my cell phone.

After a few minutes of nosing around at my pants I managed to get my muzzle into the pocket. As delicately as I could I took the edge of the phone in my teeth and tugged it free. The screen was dark and sleeping. I tapped it with my paw and the lock screen flickered into view, prompting me to "Draw your Pattern." A 3x3 block of dots filled the screen underneath.

"¡Mierda!" I cursed. I'd forgotten about that, since I usually unlocked it using the fingerprint reader on the back.

I tried to draw my pattern, but even my tiny Chihuahua paw was just too big. The phone misinterpreted my touch, losing the line or connecting the wrong dots.

As I worked cars buzzed by in the street and a few people walked by on the sidewalk, but no one noticed me or stopped to investigate.

My trembling had subsided while I worked on the phone. I lay there, head resting on my outstretched paws, trying to decide what to do. I wasn't sure what triggered it, but my skin tingled and my fur began to recede.

Branches scratched at my bare skin and tangled in my hair as I grew in size until I sat naked in the dirt, only partially concealed by the remains of the broken bush I'd been hiding under.

A car screeched to halt on the road next to me, a shocked young couple sitting in the front seats staring at me open mouthed. I smiled, gave them a little wave, and began dressing as inconspicuously as a naked woman could on a public street. A second car pulled up behind the staring couple and honked loudly several times, which jolted the driver out of their revere. The car lurched away, although not without several backward glances by the couple.

The car behind them roared off without incident. By that time I'd gotten my pants and shirt on, so all they'd seen was a disheveled woman awkwardly putting on shoes. I stuffed my underwear and bra in my mailbag. It would have taken too long to put them on and I needed to get out of here, before that couple called the cops.

I picked up my phone, wiping the dirt I'd smeared on the screen with my paws, and called my supervisor to let her know I couldn't finish the rest of my shift, making up an excuse about being violently ill. Which was true, in a way.

The next morning I called in sick, promising my livid supervisor I'd bring a doctor's note with me when I returned.

After Kirby and the kids had left for the day I turned on the computer.

I stared at the blinking cursor in the search bar. I'd had a grand plan this morning that a quick Google search would solve all my problems, but now that I was here, I realized I had no idea what to search *for*. I leaned back in my chair, drumming my fingers on the desk.

My mind flicked back to the old monster movies I'd used to watch as a kid on late-night television. Zombies, ghosts, mummies, swamp creatures, demons, devils, and, of course, werewolves. I shook my head.

I most assuredly wasn't a werewolf. I'd seen the movies. Not only did I not turn into anything close to a wolf, I wasn't violent, bloodthirsty, or out-of-control.

Plus, most importantly, I wasn't turning on a full moon. But, what was I then? The werewolf shapeshifted. *I* shapeshifted. And a dog was kinda like a wolf, right?

At a loss I typed "werewolf" into the search bar and clicked search.

The first result was, of course, Wikipedia, but scrolling through didn't yield any useful information. I clicked the back button.

The rest of the page's results were from various games and movies, so I clicked over to the second page.

"Werewolf World News" and "Cryptid Hunters" webpages made me give a startled laugh, until I remembered why I was here.

Another two hours of research brought me no closer to an answer. I tried searching for "curses," "witches," "magic," and even "lycanthropy" after reading the Cryptid Hunters webpage out of desperation. Nothing.

I slammed the mouse down in frustrated and rested my head in my hands. My hands began to shake and then my whole body vibrated. I barely had time to register what was happening before I found myself on the floor engulfed in swathes of fabric.

I dug my way out and then sat on top of my clothing with a litany of curse words, thinking of what had just happened.

A pattern had begun to emerge. Each time I'd changed I'd been angry and only changed back after calming down.

With that in mind I hopped back up into the chair and then onto the desk. The computer was still on, with Internet Explorer showing the Google homepage.

It took some trial and error of taping on the keyboard with my paws and moving the mouse around with my nose, but soon enough I managed to get the cursor back up into the search bar and typed in 'calming exercises' by pressing the keys delicately with a claw.

Half an hour of progressive muscle relaxation later found me back in human form, naked and sprawled on the couch. After I got dressed I printed posts on calming techniques until the printer ran out of ink.

I wasn't yet confident in my ability to remain calm, in-control, and, most importantly, *human* for the entire working day, however the bills wouldn't pay themselves.

I repeated my mantra meditation exercise that I'd practiced-- a *mal tiempo, buena cara* -- and headed for work.

The black lab barked at me again, but a quick reassurance that I would respect his territory boundary mollified him. He barked goodbye to me as I left.

That made me stop and smile. The dog had been more polite than most of the humans I'd had to deal with during my years of delivering mail.

Rather than ignoring the next dog on my route, I stopped, introduced myself, and explained that I was delivering mail to her owners and would leave as soon as I was done. I felt a bit silly, talking to the fluffy, white, basketball-sized poof that passed for a dog at this house, but I left the mailbox with a smile and the feeling that I'd just made the little dog's day.

By lunch time I'd actually started to enjoy myself, but then I got to Nugget's house. I scowled down at the pile of letters in my hand, debating with myself on what would happen if I just tossed them over the gate and went on with my route.

However, I didn't think "sorry, ma'am, I didn't deliver their mail because they have a tiny, ugly Chihuahua that bit me and now I turn into a dog when I get upset" would fly with my supervisor.

No sounds came from the house, but that didn't mean anything. My eyes never left the dog door as I opened the mailbox by feel, slipping the letters inside.

I backed down the walk, but nothing happened. The house was still as a tomb.

Only after the gate was latched firmly behind me did I relax with a sigh. I twisted my hands together, realizing they were shaking, so I settled down cross-legged on the sidewalk and did breathing exercises until I felt settled enough to continue on with my route.

I passed by an alley and a stray poked his head out from between two trash-cans and growled a warning at me.

"Hi there," I said, stopping, but not looking directly at the dog.

The dog's head vanished from view. I shrugged and continued on. I couldn't do anything if a dog didn't want to talk to me.

I caught sight of the stray again a few blocks away. I recognized the distinctive white spot around his eye, so I knew it was the same dog. He shadowed me for several blocks before slinking away.

My bag was empty, so I headed back to my mail truck for another load. I unlocked the door and swung the empty bag inside before climbing up after it.

"Ouch," a squeaky growl came from where the bag hit the floor.

Halfway inside already, I twisted and leaned over to grab the canvas, flinging it away to reveal Chicken Nugget crouched between the seats. I barely had time to wonder how he'd gotten inside before he lunged.

"Charge!" he howled, leaping at my face with his fangs bared.

I yelped and flinched back, flinging up my arms to protect my face from Nugget's snapping teeth. Teeth grazed my arm and he bounced off to land on the driver's side seat. The hit jolted me back and my feet slipped on the edge of the door frame. I tried to grab the seat but my hands slid right off the slick plastic covering.

My arms windmilled as I fell backwards out of the door, screaming in surprise. I landed hard on my ass on the sidewalk with my arms flung behind me. My right wrist gave a popping crack as I hit and I gasped, the shock of it sending sparks of pain all the way up my back.

I stood, but a growl from behind me made me whirl around. Four dogs advanced on me in a ragged semi-circle. I recognized two of them; the tiny, white poof-ball and the shy stray with the spot over one eye.

My inner-Chihuahua reared up, telling me not to show weakness to the pack but I couldn't help but back away until I hit the side of the truck.

Nugget appeared in the corner of my eye. He jumped out with a hop that was at once graceless and delicate. His four legs flailed through the air yet he landed lightly, like a dandelion seed buffeted by the wind, both out of control and light as a feather.

"Nugget, call off your dogs. I have nothing against you," I said, growling and showing my teeth in my best imitation of a dogs.

"Then why keep coming to all our territories, invader?" Nugget sniffed. "And then you accuse me of *cursing* you? This is to give you a lesson."

Without any further warning all five dogs advanced. A *mal tiempo, buena cara*, I chanted, trying to calm myself down. If I changed while the pack was on me I wouldn't stand a chance.

"I'm just delivering things to your humans," I said, slowly and firmly.

The white fluff-ball halted. "She was nice to me Nugget. Most of the humans don't even interact with me."

The stray cocked his head. "Fifi has a point. This human talked nicely to me earlier. We shouldn't attack her." He looked hopefully at me, tail starting to wag slowly.

The two dogs stopped and looked at Nugget, who was trembling violently, ears pinned back to his head and growling.

"But she humiliated me!" he barked.

I kept my expression serious, but inside I was smiling. The energy was leaking out of the pack. "I apologize, Nugget. I've had a bad week, but I shouldn't have tried to blame you for it."

All four dogs turned their attention towards Nugget, so I took the opportunity to sidle towards the truck door. I knew somewhere inside it would be a bad idea to turn my back on the pack, defused energy or not. I reached back, feeling out the edge of the driver's seat and then running my hand down until I felt my lunch bag.

A few quick tugs got it free. My injured wrist throbbed, but I ignored the pain as unzipped the bag and pulled out the baby carrots I always kept as a snack.

"Here you go," I said, tossing a fat carrot in the air. The stray caught it with a happy bounce in his jaws. Then I went around the ring of dogs, tossing one to each of them. They all began gnawing on the treats except for Nugget.

"I'll bring better snacks for each of you tomorrow," I said, suppressing a smile. "Consider them payment for allowing me brief access to your territory."

The stray finished his first. He cocked his head at me, lifting one ear, and then at Nugget. "Consider it done."

Fifi and then the other two dogs barked their agreement. Nugget snarled, clearly unhappy, turned up his nose at his uneaten carrot, and went racing off. The stray lunged forward and snapped up Nugget's carrot with a single crunch.

"More tomorrow?" the stray asked after he finished crunching the last carrot.

"Yes, more tomorrow," I assured him.

Fifi and the other two dogs wagged their tails, satisfied, and trotted off after Nugget. The stray came up with his ears pricked forward and sniffed me gingerly before following them.

Once I was sure they were gone I turned and stared at the truck, contemplating how I was going to finish my route with a sprained wrist.

"Wow, that was something," someone said.

The speaker was close, but huffing for breath as if they'd been jogging. I turned and looked down, but didn't see any dogs. The sidewalk in either direction was clear as well. A person cleared their throat near the hood of my truck and I jumped, looking up.

"Excuse me." A man stood at the front of the truck. He raised his arm and gave me a brief wave. He was sweating and breathing hard as if he'd just gone for a jog, although he was wearing slacks and a button-up shirt.

"Didn't mean to interrupt, but I saw how you handled that pack of dogs. I was quite impressed."

I blushed scarlet and faced him, embarrassed that I'd been so focused on looking for a dog that I'd missed him standing so close.

"Oh, well, thank you. But it was no big deal. I know most of those dogs from my route, so I already had a rapport with them," I said.

"Still," he said and shook his head. "I thought you were going to get mauled. It's why I ran over here to help, but by the time I got here you had things well in hand." He smiled and stuck out a hand. "My name's Rob."

"Hi Rob, I'm Juana." I shook hands with him and only as he pumped her arm up and down did I realize I'd unconsciously given him my injured one to shake, yet my wrist didn't hurt at all.

I glanced down at my arm, where Nugget had nipped me during his surprise attack. The scratches he had left were already gone; all that remained to of the wounds were two thin lines of drying blood. In the movies the werewolves always had amazing powers of regeneration. I resolved to reread the Cryptid website about the werewolves when I got home.

Rob was talking again and I tore my attention away from my miraculously healed arm and back to what he was saying in time to hear. "Would you consider freelance dog training?"

I blinked at him in surprise. "Dog training?"

"Yes." Rob blew out a breath. "You took those dogs from aggression to tail wagging to eating treats out of your hand in less than a minute. I've tried everything to train my dog without success, but after watching that display I'm willing to give it one more try."

"I'm sorry, I'm not--"

"I'll pay you two hundred dollars." He pulled out his wallet and showed me a wad of bills.

"I get off work in thirty minutes," I said, trying not to boggle at the amount.

The Humane Society building was a big gray, concrete building sitting out in the industrial neighborhood, squashed between warehouses and factories. My husband and I trailed behind the girls, who pushed excitedly through the glass doors ahead of us.

"Maria, Taya, slow down," I called, but they were already pelting through the lobby towards the dog viewing area.

"I'm still not sold on this," Kirby grumbled.

I smiled sweetly at him. "The girls have already promised to help, and I'll be around during the day to keep the dog out of trouble. I can even take it with me when I visit clients. You won't have to lift a finger."

"About that. I can't complain about all the extra money you're bringing in or how much calmer you've become, but," Kirby eyed her. "Where did this sudden inspiration to become a dog psychic come from anyway?"

I shrugged. "I told you. I just discovered I had this way with dogs and the rest fell into place. Now, hurry up, before the girls pick out a Great Dane or something."

We passed through the lobby and entered the area with adoptable dogs. The girls stood two kennels down from the door, cooing over a big, fluffy Husky mix.

The dogs' plaintive cries for help tugged at my heart strings and I wanted to take them all home. I did my best to tune them out.

"Remember girls, small dogs only! We don't want to scare Bella when she comes to visit."

I shooed them away from the big, fluffy dog. They moved a few kennels down and stopped.

"Wow, who's going to adopt that hideous thing?" Maria giggled, pointing at the dog further back in the cage.

"O.M.G., it's looking at me." Taya wrinkled her nose. "C'mon, let's go." She grabbed her sister and they moved off down the aisle.

I drifted over, curious to see the dog they'd so quickly rejected. A small tan Chihuahua was curled up in a tight ball against the back of the cage. It looked up as my shadow fell over it, revealing an off-center nose, an under-bite, and a comically large head with bulbous eyes.

"Chicken Nugget?" I said with a gasp. "What are you doing here?"

"Go away, human, don't taunt me about the loss of my family," he growled half-heartedly at me, the fire gone from his voice. He got up and shifted, so his back was to the front of the kennel before laying back down.

Tears pricked at my eyes. All the little dog had wanted to do was protect his family and they'd thrown him out. "I'm not here to taunt you."

"Juana, who are you talking to?" Kirby said. I jumped and fell into the chain link front of the kennel. I'd been so focused on Nugget that I'd forgotten Kirby beside me.

"I was talking to the dog," I admitted, blushing. My heart had begun to beat rapidly and I could feel the tingling tightness in my skin. I reached out and wrapped my fingers through the metal diamonds, closed my eyes, and chanted. "A mal tiempo, buena cara. A mal tiempo, buena cara."

"Is something wrong, Juana? You know I don't speak Spanish." Kirby knelt down beside me and gently touched my hand.

His touch helped me relax further. "It's an idiom. Literally it is 'when things go wrong, keep smiling.' In English I guess it is close to 'turn lemons into lemon ade.'"

To my surprise I felt the touch of a cold nose on my fingers. I'd shifted to look at Kirby while I explained my meditation mantra and when I glanced back I saw that Nugget had come over and was looking up at me with big, soulful puppy-dog eyes.

"I'm sorry that I lashed out at you." Nugget stared up at me. "I only ever wanted to protect my family."

"It's alright, Nugget," I said. I was tempted to reach a finger through to pet the end of his muzzle that still rested against my hand, but I didn't want to disrupt the fragile peace between us. "I shouldn't have tried to blame you for my problems."

Kirby snorted and I knew he'd just rolled his eyes, although I kept my gaze fixed on Nugget. "Juana, honey, the dogs are not talking to you. Save your act for your clients, ok?"

I ignored him and kept talking to Nugget. "Chicken Nugget, please accept my sincere apology for any trouble I caused you."

Nugget pricked his ears forward and wagged his tail. "I forgive you, Juana."

I suppressed a smile. He was forgiving me.

"Thank you, Nugget," I said instead.

"You are welcome, dog-human," Nugget said.

I spun on Kirby, who'd been watching me with a put-upon expression. I pointed at Nugget. "We're adopting this one."

"What?" Kirby and Nugget both responded in unison and both wrinkling their nose in distaste.

"You heard me," I said, replying to them both. "We're going to be one big happy family."

The Church Mouse

This story was originally published in *CLAW* 1 edited by Kiris and released by Furplanet in July 2018.

Anise tottered up to the votive candles, leaning heavily on her cane. The old mouse fumbled with the matches for a moment before getting one to catch. She lit a candle with a shaky paw. Then she bowed her head, closed her eyes, and whispered a brief prayer under her breath for her partner of forty years, dead as of one year ago today.

"Chandra, may the Lord watch your spirit. I miss you." Her large, round ears flattened and her whiskers twitched in grief. A single tear rolled off her muzzle. Since Chandra's death, Anise's soft, white fur had become matted and her bones showed through her skin from weight loss. Without Chandra, it had been hard for Anise to find a reason to do day-to-day activities like brush her fur or eat.

The candle she'd lit flared up, the light searing her vision. Smoke from the votive candles began to burn her eyes, and Anise turned away, almost stepping on her own tail in her haste.

Might as well go to confession while she was here. Anise tottered up the nave between the empty pews. The old mouse stopped every few steps, as much to admire the old stained-glass windows of the savior in his mouse aspect that lined the hall, as to lean over on her cane, gathering energy for the next few shuffling steps. The floorboards creaked a familiar rhythm under her claws. Her sensitive nose twitched, detecting the lingering fragrance of incense from yesterday's ceremony overlaying the smell of dust and aged wood.

Eventually, she reached the confession booth. She tucked her cane under one arm as she slid open the door. The wood paneling clattered together, comforting and familiar. The sensation lasted only as long as it took her old eyes to penetrate the gloom inside the booth and for the coppery tang of blood to slap at her nose.

A body slumped over on the bench, white fur stained red. The tip of the mouse's naked tail rested in the center of a small puddle of blood.

Anise's eyes ran up and down the body, unable to comprehend the sight before her. She let out a disbelieving squeak, and then another.

The door on the other side of the confessional booth opened with a click. "Ma'am?" the soft voice of the pastor called. Claws ticked on wood. "Is everything all right? I heard—" He gasped.

Anise staggered back, eyes never leaving the corpse. Her cane clattered to the floor. Her back claw caught on the sanctuary steps and she fell back heavily against them. Her short hairless tail came up between her skirts, the end flicking wildly in her distress.

The pastor dropped down on the steps beside her, clutching the wooden cross that hung from his neck tightly in one paw. With his other paw he crossed himself. "God save us." His eyes were fastened on the body.

Anise didn't respond. Her eyes never left the corpse's face. A face she was intimately familiar with.

"Who is it?" the pastor squeaked, his voice breaking.

Anise's heart pounded in her chest and her breaths came out in short, harsh bursts. Anise shook her head, unable to respond to the pastor's question.

The pastor turned his muzzle towards her, his eyes wide. "Ms. Pentti!"

He scrambled to his feet, claws gouging the polished wood of the sanctuary in his haste. She heard his claws clicking away from her, the bang of the rectory door, and then a moment later in the distance heard him shouting into the phone about heart attacks, dead bodies, and ambulances.

Her face never turned, her eyes never wavered from the corpse. The young mouse had died a violent death. The blue eyes were open and staring, staring straight into Anise's own. Those eyes she'd seen in the mirror countless times over her long life. The cowlick between her ears, the one she plastered down with gel every morning to keep flat, was curling up now between the dead mouse's round ears.

Anise stared into her own face, dead in the confessional booth.

The wail of an approaching siren broke Anise from her stupor. She sat up on the steps and lowered her head between her knees, gasping. The fabric of her skirt pressed against her muzzle. The familiar smell enveloped her and helped to bring her back to herself by slow degrees. Gradually she became aware of the presence of others around her.

Someone was saying, "ma'am, ma'am, can you hear me?"

"Yes. I'm fine now." Anise lifted her head and blinked at the paramedic, a large brown mouse wearing a bright blue jacket. Her pastor stood in the aisle behind the ambulance personnel wringing his paws together, his nose twitching nervously.

"We're just going to take you outside to the ambulance and make sure," the paramedic said in a soothing tone.

Anise nodded and allowed the paramedic mice to lift her onto a rolling stretcher. They wheeled her down the aisle, bodily lifting the stretcher down the stairs to the street. Once at the ambulance, they checked her blood pressure, took her temperature, and asked her a series of questions about her name, age, allergies, and such, noting down everything in their tablets.

Despite being midday on a Monday morning in the middle of a mostly residential neighborhood, the flashing lights of the cop cars had already attracted a small crowd of mice, rats, squirrels, skunks, and stoats. Anise peered past the paramedics. Patrolmen were unrolling crime scene tape around the church doors. A black rat deputy, the badge pinned to his chest sparkling in the bright morning sunlight, spoke with the pastor on the sidewalk a few feet away.

A paramedic, the brown mouse who'd spoken to her in the church, cleared his throat. "Well, Ms. Pentti, you seem to be fine from what we can tell. However, we do recommend that you let us take you in to the ER for further tests. You received quite a shock in there and at your age..."

The young mouse trailed off to silence, leaving the rest unspoken but still ringing loud and clear. *At your age you, are a delicate fucking flower, to be coddled and swaddled like a baby,* she thought. Anise rolled her eyes.

"Thank you. No, I'm fine."

She threw off the blanket they'd thrown over her and swung her legs over the side of the stretcher. Before the paramedic could protest, she slid off and onto her feet. Anise strode away, ignoring the protestations of the paramedic behind her.

"You forgot your cane, ma'am!"

Anise stopped dead in her tracks, blinking down at her empty paws and then at her legs. The pain that normally wracked her knees and legs was gone. She swished her tail in irritation as she turned to accept her cane from the helpful medic. She really wanted to check on the poor pastor, but she was still shaken from finding her younger self dead, not to mention the strange lack of pain in her legs. So instead she hurried away.

For the medic's benefit, she pretended to use the cane until she made it around the corner out of his view. Then she clutched it to her chest and sped up. Her apartment building came into view a scant few minutes later. This morning on the way to the church it had taken her over half an hour to hobble that same distance.

Anise came in through her front door and carefully hung her keys on the hook before tossing her cane into the corner. As she entered the living room, the pictures sitting on the mantle caught her eye. Something about them seemed different, but as she moved closer the rattle of dishes from the kitchen startled her. No one else should be here; since Chandra's death she'd lived alone.

"Hello?" she called, wishing she hadn't thrown her cane away from her. She crept backward, heart pounding, feeling behind herself for a weapon. "Who's there?"

Chandra, as real as life, appeared in the kitchen doorway holding a tray of steaming cinnamon rolls in oven-mitt encased paws. Her brown fur shone in the sunlight coming in through the windows, the little splotch of white fur on her chest just visible above the cut of her blouse. She looked just like she had the last time Anise had seen her.

Anise's eyes widened, her ears flared, and her tail swished back and forth behind her widely, knocking a framed picture of them together at a local street fair off the side table beside her. It hit the floor, the glass smashing against the hardwood floor with a spectacular crash, sending glass shards in every direction.

"What?" Anise managed to gasp.

"Oh, I'm so sorry." Chandra set the tray down on the dining room table and peeled off the oven mitts. Her black eyes sparkled, letting Anise know that she wasn't angry about the broken glass. "I didn't mean to startle you," she said.

"Chandra!" she finally managed to croak out. Her front paws twitched nervously; she stopped herself from rubbing them through the fur at her throat only with an effort. "But, you're dead."

"Dead?" Chandra stopped in the act of pulling a broom out of the hall closet, concern etched in the set of her pointed muzzle. She looked over at Anise's cane lying in the corner, and smile flitted briefly across her face. "So, today is the day," she whispered, mostly to herself, her paws tightening on the broom handle as she swept up the mess. She put the broom away, and then knelt down briefly in front of her bhakti shrine in the corner of the room.

Anise stepped back to give her privacy but couldn't tear her eyes from Chandra's form. She'd missed her lover so much that it hurt to not rush into her arms right then and there.

When she was done Chandra stood and turned to Anise. "Are you feeling alright?"

Anise shook her head and her muzzle split in a grin. "Yes, I'm wonderful." She danced lightly across the room and swept Chandra up in her arms, spun her about, and bent her down into a perfect ballroom dip that left them muzzle to muzzle. Chandra smelled just as Anise remembered, overlaid by sugar and cinnamon from her recent bout of cooking. No impostor then, this was Chandra, living and breathing, alive again by some miracle.

"So frisky," Chandra giggled and then licked Anise's muzzle affectionately. "Were your morning prayers so enlightening?"

"No, I've just missed you." Anise finished the dip and straightened, but kept her arms around her lover.

"You were gone all of an hour." Chandra leaned forward and gave Anise a peck on the cheek. From the kitchen a timer buzzed. She brushed her whiskers along Anise's muzzle as she pulled away. "I need to get those out before they burn."

As Chandra turned away Anise reached out and playfully grabbed her butt. Chandra giggled and gently flicked Anise's paw with the tip of her long tail from around the corner as she disappeared back into the kitchen.

Anise skipped after her. Who cared if the cinnamon rolls burned, she didn't want to miss a moment with Chandra, lest she wake from the glorious daydream. But before she reached the kitchen the doorbell rang. Anise sighed and walked over to the door. Right before she opened it she remembered to grab her cane and lean on it.

The door opened to reveal two massive brown rats dressed in perfectly pressed black suits. Her apartment building was mixed-species, both rats and mice, so the hallways were tall enough to accommodate their height, but just barely. The tips of their naked, pointed ears brushed the ceiling of the hall.

Anise kept her round ears rigid and upright, but her paws were trembling. Rats like these were government enforcers.

"Can I help you?" Anise squeaked.

In response both rats reached into their jackets and pulled out police badges. The leftmost one spoke. "I'm Detective Boom and this," he gestured to the right rat, identical almost in every way but for a notch on his muzzle, "is Detective Gruenhut. Can we come in?"

"Oh, of course, detectives." Anise limped aside, opening the door wide.

The two rats filed inside. They didn't sit, preferring to stand in the living room, looking at the pictures. Chandra appeared with a tray of steaming rolls, offering one cheerfully to each detective. They both declined, although their twitching whiskers gave away their interest.

"Detectives, this is my roommate, Chandra," Anise said, hobbling back into the living room.

Chandra gave a little nod to each of the rats, who gave her polite smiles in return. She set the tray down on the table and dusted some flour from her skirt, while shooting Anise a quizzical look.

"The detectives are here about the dead girl I found in the church this morning."

Chandra gave a little start and a squeak of surprise, her ears flattening to her head. "I'll just leave you to it then." With that she turned and scurried back into the kitchen.

Anise was grateful for the heavy smell of baked goods in the air that smothered the stench of fear that would be coming off both her and Chandra.

"Please, have a seat." Anise followed this up by sinking down into her favorite spot on the loveseat.

However, rather than sitting the rats continued looming about the room. Detective Gruenhut went over and picked up one of the framed pictures from the mantle. He held it up and squinted at it, snickered, and then passed it to his partner. Detective Boom laughed out loud. Anise racked her brain trying to remember what pictures were on the mantel and why they might be funny but couldn't think of what they might be looking at. They deliberately kept the pictures in the living room bland, things like her grandpup's school photos.

Boom grinned and shook his head. "Where's this park at? I'd love to take my pups." He flipped the picture around to show it to Anise.

Anise had to stare at it for a long moment. It wasn't a picture she'd ever seen before. The picture showed her and Chandra riding a dinosaur, horns, frills and all. Chandra had a big grin on her muzzle and was holding a frilled parasol. The dino was in a running pose, their dresses were flapping and their fur was plastered back, as if they really were moving fast.

"Ah," Anise stammered. "I don't remember."

Chandra bustled in with a tray of tea and teacups. She set the tray down on the coffee table, winking at Anise as she bent over, putting her back to the two suited rats. She straightened and smoothed her skirt. "Oh, that was in Ramoji Film City in Hyderabad."

The two rats blinked blankly at Chandra. So did Anise. She'd always wanted to take trips with Chandra as a couple. The entire idea made her heart ache at the fact that they had to keep their relationship secret from both their families.

"I'm from India. I went back to Telangana to visit my family, and Anise came along with me on holiday. Ramoji is where they film many of the Bollywood films." Chandra lifted the teapot. "Tea, anyone?"

Anise's head spun. That was a complete lie on Chandra's part. Yet, Anise could not explain the picture. This entire day just kept getting stranger.

Boom set the picture back on the mantle. "Yes, thank you," he said.

The two rats wedged themselves into the two wooden mice-sized rocking chairs while Chandra served them. Anise's china cups looked tiny in their massive paws.

Detective Boom took a sip of his tea and then lowered it. "Did you recognize the girl you found at the church today?"

Anise took a sip of her own tea, trying to think of what she should say. Thankfully, Chandra provided an excellent distraction by sitting down on the loveseat next to Anise

"Excuse me, who are you again?" Detective Gruenhut asked.

"Chandra Muni. We met in college. After Anise's husband died, she was raising three little pups all by herself and I moved in to help her out. We've been roommates ever since." Chandra gave an open muzzled smile.

"Ah." Detective Gruenhut narrowed his black eyes, staring down his long muzzle at Chandra.

Detective Boom, apparently playing the good cop today, gave a smile and continued his questions. By then Anise had settled on her story.

"Did you recognize the doe?" Detective Boom asked gently.

Anise shook her head, although her whiskers twitched, giving away her distress. "No, I'm sorry, detectives."

"She does look a lot like you," Detective Gruenhut said. "A family resemblance, if I'm not mistaken. Sure she isn't a niece or distant relative?"

Anise shrugged. Only when Chandra put a paw over her clasped fists did Anise realize she was shaking. "I know all my nieces, she isn't one of them." Anise kept her tone neutral. She was trying to keep from lying outright to the detectives.

After the two detectives were gone and Anise had shut and dead bolted the door behind them, she allowed herself to relax.

Chandra was in the kitchen, carefully washing the delicate china teacups. Anise came up behind her and wrapped her arms around the other woman from behind and pecked a kiss on one of her rounded ears. Chandra leaned back against Anise, lifting her butt to press the base of her tail firmly against Anise's crotch. Anise giggled as the tip of Chandra's tail snaked its way up her skirt and swatted her butt.

"You smell divine," Anise said, burying her nose in the ruff of fur at Chandra's neck. The cinnamon, sugar, and dough scent mixed with turmeric and own natural musk to form an intoxicating scent. She let her paws drift down over Chandra's stomach and then lower, tracing a claw in a lazy circle around Chandra's crotch over the skirt's fabric. Anise still felt as if she was in a dream, but she was determined to enjoy every second of it while it lasted.

"Careful, *jaana*. I don't want to break the china." The china teacups tinkled together as Chandra brought out a paw to flick soapy water onto Anise's nose and muzzle.

Anise leaned close and began nibbling on the edge of one of Chandra's small, rounded ears. Chandra squeaked and wrapped her tail around Anise's leg.

"Leave the dishes," Anise whispered.

Chandra pulled a paw out of the water to rub the curl of longer fur between Anise's ears. Soapy water dripped down on her face, but she didn't care.

"I already started, so I may as well finish." Chandra said as she removed her paw and went back to washing.

"I have a better idea," Anise murmured. "You keep washing dishes and I'll keep you entertained."

Anise slid down Chandra's back until she knelt behind her, then draped Chandra's skirt over her head. A few quick nips of her front teeth shredded Chandra's underwear, and the scraps of fabric fell forgotten to the linoleum. She buried her muzzle in Chandra's bottom, licking and teasing. She reached one paw up between Chandra's legs and began running a finger around Chandra's now-exposed labia. Meanwhile, she shook her other arm free of the skirt and reached up to caress Chandra's breasts, teasing at the nipple through the fabric of her shirt and bra. Chandra shuddered with pleasure.

Paws shaking, Chandra picked up a cup and carefully scrubbed it while Anise fingered Chandra's labia, running her fingers up and down the opening. She waited until Chandra rinsed the teacup and placed it in the drying rack before parting the folds of skin with her ring and index fingers, soaking her middle finger when she placed it inside. She traced small circles around Chandra's clit, occasionally flicking the bundle of nerves.

Chandra thrust her butt back into Anise's muzzle and Anise used the movement to tighten her tail around Chandra's leg. The fingers of her other paw continued to rub Chandra's nipple while she teased the nub of Chandra's clit.

Grasping the edge of the sink with her breaths coming in ragged gasps, Chandra had given up all pretense of washing dishes. Anise could feel Chandra's wet desire slicking her pads, so she adjusted her paw, cupping her fingers to slip them up inside Chandra. Her thumb stroked the clit while she drove three of her fingers in and out of Chandra with increasing intensity.

Anise lapped at Chandra's vulva, running her tongue along the sensitive skin and then up around the tight, puckered flesh of her anus.

A moan from Chandra turned into a shriek of pleasure as Chandra's vagina spasmed around Anise's fingers.

The next morning, Anise woke Chandra with sweet kisses. A year of waking to a cold bed left her even more appreciative of what she'd been missing. They had sex again, this time with Chandra on top, and then lay for over an hour snuggling together in the bed.

Much later, Chandra finally dragged them out of bed, first she said her daily morning prayers at her shrine and then made them a big pancake breakfast topped with strawberries from their window box.

"So, why'd you lie to those detectives, *jaanu?*" Chandra asked as they were washing the breakfast dishes.

Anise's paws started trembling and she dropped the dish she was drying. The plate smashed on the floor.

"Ah, I didn't mean to startle you." Chandra grabbed the broom and began sweeping up the pieces.

"How did you know I was lying? Oh, god, did those detectives know, too?" Anise leaned on the counter.

"No, well, yes, but it's complicated." Chandra dumped the contents of the dustpan into the garbage. "Do you want to talk about it?"

"I-I'll sound crazy." Anise picked back up the hand towel and began drying the pan.

"I assure you, you won't." Chandra put the broom back in the closet, brushing Anise's legs with her tail as she walked behind her.

Chandra led her into the living room and they curled up on the couch together, twining their tails. Anise told Chandra all about yesterday morning, starting with her lightning a votive candle for the anniversary of Chandra's death.

"I know." Chandra said as Anise finished up her story.

"You do?" Anise shook her head. "I'm not sure I believe myself and I was there." She jerked her head to meet Chandra's gaze. "How is it you say you know? Also, when did we get that picture taken, anyway? I've never been with you to visit your family."

Chandra ruffled the fur between Anise's ears. "That's a secret for now. I wish I could say more, but I can't. Not yet."

"Wait, what?" Anise protested, but Chandra held a finger up against the end of Anise's muzzle.

"That reminds me," Chandra said, unwinding herself from their pile on the couch and offering Anise a paw up. "I have something to show you."

She led Anise into their spare bedroom. As part of their cover, Chandra kept her clothes and personal effects in this room, although she slept in Anise's bed every night. From underneath the bed, Chandra pulled out a whiteboard covered in clipped articles and colored marker lines. Looking at the dates, some were over a hundred years old and others were dated for the future, but all the papers looked crisp and new.

"Wh--what is this?" Anise said, staring at the board with wide eyes. As she read the articles, she noticed a common theme: all of them were about the church.

"After you save me, this is the work we'll be doing," Chandra said, her eyes shining.

"But, you're already saved?" Anise asked. "And this, what is it that we'll be doing?"

Chandra shook her head while picking up her tail and fiddling with the end of it. "I'm not saved yet, but you will save me, and soon. As for our work, we're going to start a group to break the hold of the church, separating it from politics."

"Um," Anise raised a paw. "Why?"

"Let me ask something. Where was I buried?" Chandra dropped her tail and took Anise's paw in hers.

Anise frowned and looked away. "India," she whispered, unable to stop her ears from flattening and her tail tip from twitching. "In Telangana, in your family plot. That's why I lit the candle for you, instead of going to your grave. We were together forty years, yet I had no say in anything."

"I don't blame you, " Chandra said softly, before her voice got a hard tone. "I blame the system, the influence of the church, for why we have to hide our love for one another."

"What does that have to do with what happened yesterday?" Anise's head spun. She sunk down on the bed, shoving the whiteboard aside to make room.

"Yesterday morning is when the church sends your past self to kill you. You have to go back and stop her," Chandra said.

"But she's already been stopped." Anise groaned and put her muzzle into her paws. This was all so confusing.

"No, but she will be." Chandra said.

"How?"

"By you, of course." Chandra looked at the clock on the wall. "This afternoon. We should get going. Don't want you to be late." Chandra paused and then added.

"After you save yourself, don't forget to come back in time to save me."

"But how will I do that? And won't they just come looking for you again?"

Chandra smiled and shook her head. "You'll know how to do it when you get there. Trust me, your plan will be brilliant." She winked at Anise and then pecked her on the cheek.

Anise and Chandra walked up to the church steps. Anise gripped her cane tightly and glanced at Chandra.

"What do I do?"

"Go inside. You'll figure it out." Chandra turned to go.

"You're leaving?" Anise's ears flattened.

"I can't help you here. In your timeline, you haven't saved me yet. I'll be at home, waiting for you, when you're done." Chandra walked away, her round ears ramrod straight, her heels clicking on the sidewalk and her tail twitching giving away how worried she really was.

Anise took a deep breath and slowly made her way up the stairs. As she walked the light changed, the shadows shifted, until the stairs were in pre-dawn shadow. She'd stepped back in time, to early morning the day before. She wasn't sure how she'd done it, or how she knew with such certainty that she'd just stepped through the veil to travel back in time, but she trusted this new knowledge implicitly.

Inside the church, everything was still and quiet. No other parishioners were about at this early hour.

Confession didn't officially start until nine, when her past self would arrive. The votive candles were just as she remembered from the day before, except for one detail. Anise grabbed a match and lit a candle, giving thanks to God for Chandra's return. Now it was just as she remembered.

Anise walked about up the nave, her confident steps echoing off the walls of the church. She swung her cane, tapping on the floor only when it suited her.

She stopped at the confession booth and opened the door. Empty, as it should have been the day before. So where was the young version of herself?

There was a creak from the front doors. Anise slipped into the booth and held the door so that it shut quietly. She sat down on the bench, gripping her cane between her paws, trying to think. She wasn't going to kill her past self, but then, what was she going to do?

The door to the booth opened. Anise jumped to her feet, raising her cane like a baseball bat. Detective Boom grinned back at her.

"Hah, so it was you. Put that cane down, I'm not going to hurt you."

"Why are you here?" Anise narrowed her eyes, lifting her cane higher.

"I'm here to help you. Give you your welcome." Boom gestured and stepped to the side.

Detective Gruenhut slid his arm around Boom and pecked him on the cheek.

"Wait, you aren't really with the government, are you?" Anise set down her cane.

"No," Boom grinned at Gruenhut, who grinned back. "We're here to help."

"But Chandra said--"

"We were already both saved." Boom said as Gruenhut pulled away. "Now, some ground rules. We can give you advice, instructions, answer questions, but we can't do the deed. It's gotta be you."

Gruenhut nodded to the cane in Anise's shaking paw. "That the only weapon you have with you?"

"Weapon? Uh," she glanced at the two big rats still looming over her, blocking the only way out of the booth. If they wanted to hurt her, she mused, they already could have. "Yes, this is it."

"Here," Gruenhut reached one of his massive paws into his suit jacket. Anise squeaked and shrank back against the back of the booth. He pulled his paw out to reveal a tiny, mouse-sized gun. "You're shaking."

"Why me?"

"You were targeted by the Cross Auream, a secret society the church uses to eliminate the," Broom held up his paws and made air quotes, "gay problem."

"I expected them to come for me after they got Chandra, but it had been over a year. I thought- well, I didn't know. Maybe she didn't give me up?"

Boom shook his head. "She did, but you were slated for an experimental program."

"Apparently involving time travel."

"Yes," Boom said, glancing about. "But we're out of time."

Gruenhut held out the little pistol towards Anise. "You ever used one of these?"

Anise shook her head, almost numb as she took the pistol from Gruenhut. "No."

He pointed to parts of the gun. "This is the trigger. This little push-button on the handle is the safety. Gun won't fire if you aren't holding it down tight. Don't point the business end at anything you don't intend to shoot."

"Good luck." Boom said, lumbering away.

Gruenhut gave Anise a little salute. "See you on the other side."

"Wait," Anise said. "What do I do?"

"Kill or be killed."

Anise gripped the gun firmly. She peeked out of the booth and the two rats were gone. She just caught sight of Gruenhut's tail as it disappeared through the door at the back of the chapel that led to the offices. Just as the door clicked shut behind him, the front entrance creaked open.

Not wanting to be surprised again, Anise eased the door to the booth shut, leaving it cracked just enough for her to see. A slim form stepped through the door, pastel skirt swirling around her legs and showing off her high-heeled pumps. Anise recognized her instantly. Her younger self. From the sway of her hips and the sparkle in her eyes, she was her from right before the wedding. The sensation was surreal, like looking in a mirror at her past. She had a sensation of déjà vu, as if she's seen this before, long ago in a since forgotten memory.

Anise shook her head to clear it and focused on the present, forcing herself to focus on the gun sensation of the gun in her paw. Scowling in disgust, she tucked it into her skirt pocket. This was herself. She couldn't shoot a past version of herself. The thought made her fur stand on end. She took her cane back up, opened the door to the booth, and came hobbling out.

"Hello, dearie," she said as young Anise turned to look at her.

Young Anise looked her up and down, lips peeling up. "Ewww, I got so old."

Anise frowned. "With age comes wisdom. Why are you here?"

"I'm here to keep myself from making the same mistakes as you. They came to see me. Warned me that in the future I become," her eyes narrowed in disgust, "a lesbian."

"That doesn't answer my question." Anise took a few hobbling steps down the nave towards her Younger self. "Why are you *here*? Who sent you?"

"The Aureum. I need to kill you, my lesbian future, to stop it from happening." Young Anise took a gun from her pocket of her skirt, holding it loosely by her side.

"And if you don't?"

"They kill me. And I *won't* miss my wedding tomorrow, for anything." Young Anise lifted the gun and pointed it straight at Anise.

Anise's heart sank. She remembered the time leading up to her wedding. She'd put her heart and soul into planning it down to the last detail. She'd been so excited, she would have killed if someone had tried to take it away from her.

Young Anise put her other paw on the gun and sighted down the barrel. Anise ducked and rolled between the pews just as the gun barked. Young Anise's shoes clicked on the floor as she ran down the nave. Anise laid down, scrambling under the pews towards the front of the church. She slid her cane out into the nave just as the Young her came running up. The girl squeaked in shock as she tumbled face first to the ground, snapping one of the heels off her expensive pumps. Her little gun popped free of her paw and skittered away.

Honestly, Anise thought as she stood and took her own pistol out of her pocket, *who wears heels to go kill someone?* She closed her eyes and turned her head away.

From this range Anise couldn't miss.

The shot was still reverberating from the windows when the office door opened, and Boom and Gruenhut appeared. They helped her carry the body over and hide it in the nave where she'd first discovered it.

While Boom and Gruenhut cleaned up the blood, Anise retrieved her Younger version's gun. To her surprise, the gun was identical to the one that the rats had given her, right down to the serial number etched onto the barrel. Or, as she reflected, maybe it shouldn't have surprised her at all.

Boom and Gruenhut offered to walk her back to the apartment.

"What did I accomplish back there?" Anise asked them as they strolled along.

"To change the future, you have to change the past," Gruenhut said.

"Is that what the young me meant?"

"Time isn't a stream or a river," Boom said with a shrug. "Those targeted by the Cross Aueram, if they manage to kill their future self, can change their future. Think of time more as a lake. Ripples in the future extend out in every direction."

Anise shuddered. The thought of being forever stuck in a marriage to a man she wasn't attracted to, never meeting Chandra. "How horrible. But then, what happens to me? I killed my younger self—"

Boom shrugged. "Honestly? We can tell you our theory, but that's about it."

"Alright," Anise hedged. "So I take it the same thing happened to both of you?"

"Well, to Boom here first, then he got me," Gruenhut said, giving Boom a friendly punch on the arm. Anise noticed that he and Boom were just as careful as she and Chandra to avoid physical affection while out in public.

"So, what's your theory?"

"Well, you killed your past self, but you still have all your memories and the past didn't actually change, see?" Boom said. "Like, we went to the library and looked up newspaper archives. Nothing was different."

Anise nodded. "A paradox. That's why I had to be the one to kill my younger self. If one of you killed her, she'd have been dead along with me."

"Right," Gruenhut said. "We're living paradoxes. It's why we think we can move through time, and stuff."

"Ah, like why my joints don't hurt anymore or I don't need my cane."

"Gruenhut and I, we go to thinking about how to best use these powers," Boom said with a grin.

"The whiteboard," Anise whispered to herself. Louder, to Boom and Gruenhut, she said, "you want to stop the Cross Aueam."

"Exactly!" Boom whooped. "So, you in?" He stuck out his arm, holding his massive paw in front of her.

"I'm in." Anise grinned up at him as she set her tiny paw in his big one. "We just have one stop to make first. I have to save Chandra."

Bucking the Trend

This story was originally published in *The Furry Cookbook* edited by Thurston Howl and released by Thurston Howl Publications in 2019.

Theo closed the app on his phone, tapping so hard his hoof-tipped finger almost broke the screen. Then, for good measure, he tossed it across the room, aiming for his bed where it bounced off the pillow. He was mad, yes, but not angry enough to risk ruining his expensive phone.

Why did online dating have to be so hard? Why were guys such jerks? It was Friday, damn it. He should be getting ready for a hot date with a hot buck, not sitting alone in his bedroom.

Absently, he reached up to scratch his antler attachments. The surgery had been six months ago. They were healing nicely, but they still itched.

He glanced around the small room and spotted his phone laying on top of his empty backpack. His eyes ran over a poster on his wall that showed a green, leafy forest. On impulse he grabbed the empty bag and started stuffing clothing into it. It might be October, but it hadn't gotten that cold yet. He was going camping.

On his way out the door he snagged some butter out of the fridge and then an acorn squash and a few onions out of the garden, stuffing them into his pack on top of his clothes.

He opened his car door and tossed his bag into the passenger seat before ducking down to slide into the driver's side. He didn't duck low enough for the height of his new antlers and they bounced off the doorframe, painfully pulling at his new scars.

"Ouch," he snarled, standing back up and rubbing at the top of his head. "Stupid things." He grabbed the base and twisted, detaching one antler and then the other. He tossed them onto the passenger seat next to his backpack and then got behind the wheel.

He wove out of the city and then headed up a canyon into the mountains. As the green trees whipped by the windows, he could feel himself starting to relax. This had been a good idea. There was a pull off ahead near a trailhead. About ten miles up the trail were some camp sites he'd used before that were first come, first serve. This time of the year there shouldn't be anyone else up there.

He parked and got out of the car, shivering as the cold air hit the fur on his arms. Ever since he started testosterone he'd been warmer and been having to wear less layers, but he still had emergency sweatshirts stashed everywhere he frequented. He got a hoodie out of the back seat and pulled it on over his head, reflecting as he did so that there were benefits to removable antlers. His cis-guy friends all had to buy zip-up hoodies and button-up shirts because they couldn't get the pull-over stuff over their antlers.

Speaking of antlers, Theo pulled his off the passenger seat and reattached them before shrugging on the backpack. This time of year there wasn't much birdsong, but even the sound of the wind rustling through the leaves around him as he hiked relaxed him still further.

His hooves and legs were sore from the hike up by the time he reached the campsite at the top of the rise. As he predicted he had his pick of spots. Only one other tent was visible, pitched at the far end of the camp site and almost hidden by the trees. In his haste Theo hadn't packed a tent, but the weather forecast was clear.

He set his bag down in a camping spot and went to gather twigs and logs to start a campfire. It wasn't long before his fire was merrily burning away in the brick fire pit closest to the spot he'd picked away from the other camper. There was only one pit for every four campsites, not that that was an issue tonight.

He pulled out the squash and set it on the bricks by the fire to warm up. Then with a stick he pushed a burning log away to make room for the two onions. He put them inside the pit, as far from the fire as he could get them, nestled up against the brick edge of the pit. Almost immediately the scent of roasting onion wafted up from their skins where they rested against the hot bricks.

Now that the squash was warm, he pulled out his big pocket knife and rolled the squash onto its side, preparing to cut the top off. Just as he was slashing down with the knife, a deep male voice came out of the darkness behind him.

"Wow, that smells good."

Theo jumped in surprise and his knife missed the top of the squash. The blade bounced off the bricks with a ping, putting a big dent in the edge. Theo turned to glare at the newcomer, ready to give him a piece of his mind, but instead his mouth just opened and closed uselessly. The stranger had moved closer, giving Theo a good view of him in the light of the fire. The stranger turned out to be the most handsome buck Theo had ever seen with long lashes, big black eyes, and soft-looking tan fur that Theo wanted to run his fingers through. The buck wore a zip-up black jacket and jeans.

"Gah," was all Theo managed to spit out.

The stranger leaned closer, closing his eyes and flaring his nostrils. "Is that onion and squash?"

"Uh, yeah," Theo finally got out. What was this about? Why was this buck drooling over his food?

"It smells delicious." The buck opened his eyes, flashed Theo a smile, and crossed his legs to settle down next to Theo. "Mind if I sit with you?"

Theo's eyes widened. "I, uh, no. I don't mind," he stuttered out.

Picking back up his knife, Theo sighed over the damage to the blade. Ruined. But it still should be sufficient to cut the top off his squash. He wiped the blade off on his pants and then sawed off the top of the squash. Setting aside the top, he used the knife to scoop out the seeds and then plopped the cube of butter from his bag into the opening. He set the top back on and then nestled the squash into the ashes in front of his roasting onions. Normally he'd hold it on with toothpicks, but in his haste to leave the house he'd neglected to pack any. However, he'd cut it at an angle, and that was enough to keep the top from falling inside.

"What are you doing?" the stranger asked, cocking his head as he watched. "Don't you need a pan or something?"

"Nope," Theo said, using the knife tip to carefully rotate the onions so that they cooked evenly. "You can cook them directly in the fire. Once they're done, you just peel the skins off and eat the insides." He lay the pocketknife in the dirt next to him, since with the blade bent he couldn't flip the blade back into the handle, and turned to the stranger, holding out a hand. "I'm Theo, by the way."

"Lukas," the buck replied, reaching out and firmly shaking Theo's proffered hand. His hoof-tipped fingers scrapped Theo's as Lukas withdrew. A thrill went down Theo's spine and the urge to flee from this handsome buck became nearly overwhelming. Behind him his tail popped up flagging white with his fear, and Theo was glad it was dark so Lukas couldn't see how nervous he was.

It was dark enough now that he could no longer see the tent through the trees, but he pointed in the direction he thought it was. "That your tent?"

"Yeah," Lukas sighed and leaned back to rest on his hands. "Being October I thought I'd be the only one out here."

"Me, too," Theo admitted, wondering again why, if the stranger had come up here to be alone, he'd come over to join Theo at his fire.

"Your onions smell delicious," he said, as if he'd heard Theo's unasked question.

Theo shrugged, but inside he was smiling. They really did smell great. "Thanks—"

His reply was cut off by a loud growl coming from Lukas' stomach. The lining of the handsome buck's ears turned pink and he glanced away, putting a hand up to his stomach.

"Um, would you like to share my meal?" Theo asked. It would have been too much just for himself anyway. He'd been planning to save the second onion and part of the squash for breakfast, but he could just wait till he got back to the city to eat. "Were you not able to get dinner before you came camping?"

"It's uh, kinda a long story." Lukas leaned forward to rest his face in his hoof-hands, causing Theo to have to dodge to the side to avoid having one of the long tines coming from the far end of Lukas' rack snagging on his hoodie. Lukas noticed his flinch and groaned, scooting his butt over a few inches on the dirt and tilted his head away. "You're lucky yours are so small," Lukas grumbled.

Actually, Theo had begged his surgeon to give him bigger antlers, but she'd stood firm. Smallest model attachments only for the first year, to give the implants time to heal properly and for him to get used to the extra weight on his head. "Uh, y-y-yeah," was all he managed to stammer out.

To cover his embarrassment he picked up his knife and pushed up so that he could give all three of the roasting vegetables a turn so that they cooked evenly. When he was done he settled back down at an angle, turned more towards Lukas, but not so far that he couldn't keep an eye on his cooking. "Well, it's going to be at least another hour before these are done. I'll tell you my story, if you tell me yours. Deal?" Theo held out a hoof-hand towards Lukas, who was still slumped over hiding his face in his hooves.

"Fine." Lukas reached up and shook Theo's hoof without looking up. "You first."

"Fine," Theo groaned. It had been his idea to pass the time this way, after all. "I'm up here to get away from everyone because, well, I'm frustrated that I haven't been on a date in two years. It's Friday night, I should be at a club with a hot doe or a handsome buck, not sitting at home alone watching reruns of Doctor Hooves." Now Theo mimicked Lukas' pose, hiding his face. He hadn't meant to admit to quite so much. Especially about his geeky love of the Doctor. Well, might as well throw it all out there now. "And yes, I know I could just go to the club by myself. But I've tried that. It's boring. And no one looks twice at a tiny little, uh, buck like me."

He risked a glance out through his hooves at Lukas. The bigger buck had straightened back up, resting his hoof-hands in his lap. He was giving Theo a confused look. "So," Lukas said, "you didn't want to be home alone tonight, so you came up here to. . . be. . . alone?"

"Well, when you put it like that," Theo sighed and absent-mindedly ran a hoof along the base of an antler. "I don't know why I came up here. I just wanted to clear my head, I guess. Not worry about being dateless for the thousandth night in a row."

"Makes sense," Lukas said with a nod.

Theo turned and checked on the onions and poked the squash, giving them each another quarter turn before settling back down and looking at Lukas. "Your turn."

"It's stupid," Lukas said, drawing in the dirt to his side with a hoofed finger.

"Stupider than coming up to the mountains to be alone because I didn't want to be at home, alone?" Theo snorted.

That drew a belly laugh from Lukas. "Actually, yes. It is." He fell silent, staring into the fire.

Theo sat quietly, waiting while Lukas gathered up the nerve to speak. Beside him sap in the branches he'd gathered snapped and popped. The wind rushed through the unseen branches overhead, and blew straight through Theo's thin hoodie. He shivered and rubbed his arms with his hoof-hands, scooting closer to the fire.

"Oh, are you cold?" Lukas asked. "I have an extra hoodie in my tent."

Theo shivered and said through clacking teeth, "Sure."

"Be right back." Lukas got to his feet and stumbled away into the dark. Branches snapped and he heard Lukas cursing. He wondered why such a prepared hiker, one with extra warm clothes and a nice tent, didn't seem to have basics like food or a flashlight. Not that he was any better prepared.

Theo tended to his cooking while he waited for Lukas to return. A few minutes later cracking branches and muttered curses heralded Lukas' return. He plopped down next to the fire and wordlessly handed Theo a zip-up sweatshirt that smelled like mud and, even in the dim light of his campfire, looked none too clean. No matter. Warmth was warmth. It was actually good that it was far too big for him, because he was easily able to put it on overtop his other sweatshirt and still have room to zip it up. He pushed up the too-long sleeves. "Thanks."

Lukas' teeth flashed in the dim light. "You're welcome. Least I can do in trade for the first meal I'll be having in days."

"Wait, days?" Theo stared at the buck. Now that he thought about it, he hadn't seen any other cars parked in any of the lots or along the road on his way up here. Had he hiked here from somewhere else?

"Yeah," Lukas ducked his head again and looked away. "I've wanted to hike the Pacific Crest Trail for ages. I'm planning to do full trail starting next spring. This trip is kind of a practice run. I was supposed to hike from Seattle down to Portland, then catch the train back home."

Now it was Theo's turn to look confused. "Supposed to?"

"Well, uh, I kind of ran into a snag."

"You ran out of food, didn't you." Theo chuckled as he crossed his arms and shook his head.

"Yeah." The buck hung his head. "I did," he whispered.

"You know it's another fifty miles to Portland," Theo said, thinking of how long it had taken him just to drive up here. Without food, Lukas would never make it the three or four more days it would take him to hike in. "I can give you a ride to the train station in the morning."

"That'd be great," Lukas said with a groan, pulling his knees to his chest and resting his chin on them.

"What about your flashlight? I noticed you stumbling around in the dark. Did you forget it?"

"Ran out of batteries. Those things are heavy, but I guess I skimped a little too much. I should have taken the clerk up on that purchase of a solar-charged battery pack after all." Lukas sighed.

Theo leaned over and patted Lukas' leg as he sat up to check on the cooking, before picking up his bent knife. He poked at the flesh of the acorn squash with the flat of the blade and it easily dented the side. The squash was done. He set the knife down on the edge of the fire pit and used the fingertips of each of his hoof-hands to pick up the hot squash on either side. The thick keratin nubs at the ends of each finger weren't affected by the heat. He set the squash on the bricks and then check the onions, which were browned to perfection. He carefully picked up each one and set them on either side of the squash.

Next Theo grabbed the squash's stem and lifted off the top. Steam and a strong aroma of roasted squash and butter rolled out of the opening. Lukas' head popped up and his big nostrils flared.

Theo closed his eyes and inhaled deeply, salivating at the scent. This was the best part of any meal. He heard Lukas shifting around and then felt the heat of his body as he pressed close to Theo. Theo opened his eyes and glanced over at Lukas. The buck was even more handsome up close, if that were possible. But now that he was closer to Theo and the light of the fire, he could see the dirt marking the buck's fur and see the big black circles under his eyes.

"Here, that onion is yours," Theo picked up the knife and gently tapped the head of the onion closest to Lukas. "Peel off the outer layers and then you can just eat the inside like an apple."

Lukas grabbed the onion. "Hot, hot," he juggled it back and forth for a moment before he was able to get a grip with his fingertips. Steam billowed out as he peeled back the outer layers. Lukas didn't even wait until he had the whole thing done, as soon as there was enough room to take a bite he began chomping at the onion's soft, white insides.

While Lukas devoured his onion, Theo used the knife to cut the acorn squash in half. Butter ran over his hands and scalded his palms. He used the blade of the knife to clumsily scoop out the seeds. Belatedly he realized that Lukas probably had utensils like spoons in his tent that would have made this job easier. He turned to Lukas intending to ask, but the buck was so engrossed in his food that Theo just shrugged and finished up as best he could with the knife.

He held up Lukas' half of the acorn squash as the buck was finishing up the last few bites of his onion. Lukas' eyes lit up and he tossed the onion peel aside to take the squash.

"Just like the onion, peel off the outside and eat," Theo said as he passed the golden squash over to Lukas. The outside of the squash was singed since it was closer to the fire, but that didn't matter because you generally didn't eat the skin anyway.

By the time Theo had finished speaking, Lukas had already stuck the end of his muzzle into the squash and taken a big bite right from the center. Lukas mumbled something unintelligible around a mouthful of squash and kept eating.

Theo laughed and picked up his own squash half. Peeling back the skin on one edge, Theo took a big bite. Normally he would have added salt and pepper at this stage, or even some cinnamon, rosemary, and maple syrup if he had a sweet tooth that day, but even with just butter the squash's flesh melted in his mouth. Theo took his time, savoring each bite. He'd only eaten about half of his piece when Lukas let out a big sigh and laid down onto his back. The tines of his antlers dug into the dirt behind him.

"That was the best meal I've ever had."

Theo chewed and swallowed, then laughed. "I think that's just your starvation talking."

"No way, man." Lukas closed his eyes and patted his belly. "Delicious."

"Well, thanks."

Lukas lay there in contented silence as Theo finished eating. He thought the bigger buck had fallen asleep. After he'd cleaned up the discarded squash and onion skins by tossing them in the fire to burn, he leaned over Lukas, intending to shake him gently awake. The buck's eyes snapped open before Theo even touched him. Theo froze as Lukas met his gaze.

Smiling, the buck rolled on his side and propped his head up with one hoof-hand to look at Theo, who was still frozen with indecision. "I noticed you don't have a tent."

Theo gulped. "No," he whispered. "It's nice enough. I was just going to sleep under the stars." He shivered as a gust of cold wind blew through all his layers and ruffled the fur of his chest.

Lukas' smile widened and he reached forward with his other hand to pull the zipper of the hoodie he'd loaned Theo up until it rested snuggly against his throat. "Your choice," he winked. "But my tent is big enough for two."

Heat flooded Theo's cheeks and he fell back to land on his rump. He watched speechless, as Lukas stood up and stretched slowly then strutted off into the dark in the direction of his two-deer tent. Theo's eyes fixed on Lukas' ass, nicely defined by his hiking jeans. His white-edged tail protruded out above his shorts, waving like a flag and highlighting the soft curves of Lukas' rear-end. It would have been a glorious exit as he vanished into the dark, except that it was immediately followed by a loud curse and a thud, then Lukas said from the dark, "I'm ok. Antlers just caught in a branch."

Theo shook his head as he got to his hooves, able to follow Lukas' trip back to the tent by the sounds of snapping branches and muffled curses. He looked at the dwindling fire and then at his own tiny backpack sitting next to an empty space on the dirt. He did have a thin, rolled up camping mat in his bag, but he knew from experience just how thin it really was. Lukas probably didn't have anything cushier, having to haul everything on ones back meant packing light, but he did have a tent to protect against some of this arctic wind.

And then there was Lukas himself. The buck was very hot, and had made his interest very clear. However, Theo was nervous how the buck would react to finding out he was trans. Plus, well, he wasn't sure he actually wanted to have sex with Lukas, even as hot as he was. He shivered again and realized he should take Lukas up on the offer of the warmer tent. So far Lukas hadn't been pushy and seemed to respect boundaries. He'd go, at least, and see how it went. His instinct was that if he asked to stop, Lukas would respect that.

Nervously, Theo picked up his bag and began feeling his way towards Lukas' tent. When he got there he could hear the buck rooting around inside. Theo tried to knock on the tent wall, but his fist just made a whooshing sound on the fabric. "Hello, Lukas?"

There was a sound of a zipper opening. All of a sudden light spilled out of something in Lukas' hand, blinding Theo. He fell back with a cry, covering his eyes.

"Oh, sorry." The blinding light dimmed somewhat. Theo blinked against the glare to see Lukas holding up a tiny lantern. "I found one more battery. Guess it had gotten rolled into that hoodie I loaned you. Come in, come in."

Theo awkwardly climbed inside, careful not to catch his antlers on the fabric. Not that it mattered. The area around the zipper and the top of the tent were covered in a variety of small puncture marks that had been crudely patched with duck tape. He sat his bag down and crawled to the side so that Lukas could zip the tent shut. Theo already felt considerably warmer. He unzipped Lukas' hoodie and took it off, tossing it onto a pile of Lukas' things on one end of the tent.

Lukas set the lantern on the floor of the tent and then moved to sit next to Theo. "You came," he said with a smile.

"Yes, but uh, there's something I have to tell you first." Theo said quickly, trying to quash down his nervousness. Lukas deserved to know before things went any further.

"Oh?" Lukas sat back and turned to fully face Theo, crossing his legs. "Does it have to do with you being trans? Cause I already figured it out, back at the fire."

"You did?" Theo stared at him, mouth gaping open. "How?"

Lukas gestured at Theo's pull over hoodie. "Dead giveaway, dude. First thing you should do, if you want to pass better, get rid of all your pull-overs and buy zip-ups. Cis-guy whitetails don't buy pull-overs, they wouldn't be able to get them on for half the winter until their antlers fell off."

"Of course." Theo let out a laugh of half relief and half wonderment. Not only was Lukas taking it really well, he was giving Theo tips on passing. "Wait," Theo gave Lukas a startled glance. "You knew when you flirted with me? You don't mind?"

"I don't mind. I like guys, and you're cute." Lukas held up a hand. "Also, I swear this is not a pity fuck after hearing your story. Those guys and girls who turned you down don't know what they're missing. You're adorable, a great cook, and an excellent listener."

Theo felt his ears and muzzle getting warm as he blushed. "Oh."

"Plus," Lukas lowered his voice conspiratorially, "I'm kind of jealous you can take your antlers off when they get in the way." He glanced up at the duck-tape covered top of his tent.

Theo let out a laugh. "It is kinda convenient," he admitted. A thrill went through him and he leaned down to plant a kiss on Lukas' nose. Right then, the lantern flickered and died, plunging them into darkness. Lukas must have moved, because Theo's muzzle landed right against the end of Lukas'. He didn't protest as Lukas pulled him in for a long kiss.

The Pine Lesson

This story was originally published in *Ironclaw: The Book of Legends* released by Sanguine Games in July 2020.

Espen approached the librarian with trepidation. His hooves clicked softly on the wooden floor, despite his best efforts to walk quietly. The squirrel librarian sat bent over a book behind her desk, her fluffy brown tail curled behind her head, but she looked up and smiled at him as he approached.

"How can I help you?"

Espen ran a hand through his forelock nervously. "I have a question about elementals."

One of the librarian's dark eyebrows rose, but she merely nodded her head for him to continue.

"We learned how to speak to them last week in class. I've been trying to practice on the elemental I found, but I can't get it to respond." With this Espen reached into his bag, pulled out his most prized possession, and set it on the desk in front of her. It was a small sprig of pine of a type not found it in his southern homeland of

Avoirdupois, which was why he had originally picked it up when he'd stumbled across it as a young colt. He'd immediately felt the magic radiating from it, although he hadn't had a word for it at the time. In a way it had led him here, leaving home to study magic at Dunwasser College.

The librarian leaned over her desk to peer at the twig, her black nose twitching. After a moment, she sat back up and shook her head. "I'd wager to say it's not talking to you because it's not an elemental."

"It's not?" Espen stared down at the stick in shock. "Then what is it?"

Her tail jerked and twitched behind her as she thought for a moment. "I'm not sure," the squirrel woman said finally, "but I have some ideas where you can start looking." She stood up and gestured for Espen to follow her.

They wove their way through the stacks, only passing one other student, an upper-level fox student in red robes. She was studying fire magic, while Espen's plain brown robes with the yellow bands indicated he was a first year studying earth magic. Eventually the librarian stopped in front of a large bookcase.

"Here you go," the squirrel said, gesturing at the books.

Espen stared at the giant bookcase in despair. "All these?"

The librarian shrugged. "Plant is a pretty broad thing to be searching for, without something else to narrow it down. Library closes at dusk. Good luck in your search, young horse." With that she turned and left.

Espen scanned the titles on the shelves, shaking his head. This was going to take forever. He chose a book, mostly at random, and carried it over to the closest table. He gave up after three pages. The author assumed that the reader had a lot more magical knowledge than Espen had. He returned the book to the shelf and picked another one.

This time instead of picking at random, he carefully read the titles. He found a volume about how to use magic to better grow plants and took it over to the table.

The book's title had given him a much better idea about how to figure out what his sprig was. He knew grapevines could be regrown from a cutting, so perhaps other plants could be as well. After it was regrown, it would be quicker than a tail snap to identify what it was. It was almost dusk by the time he was ready. He had found a spell in the book that did exactly what he needed, but with his limited knowledge of magic it had taken a while to untangle the spell. As a first-year student, he was only allowed to check out books from the front, beginner-level shelves, or else he would just take this book back to his room to try the spell there.

Espen took the stick out of his pocket and set it on the table. Then he held one hand over the stick, using the other to keep track of his place in the spell, and began repeating the words while channeling his magic out through his palm. The stick jumped, dancing as the magic hit it. When Espen finished reciting the words to the spell, the sprig fell back to the table, lifeless and looking no different, and Espen sat back with a frown, canting one ear back. He was sure he'd cast the spell properly.

Then the stick shivered and began to grow. And grow. Espen let out a little neigh of dismay, snatching the library book from the table and jumping backwards. His chair fell over with a loud clatter. He clutched the book to his chest as he watched the twig, grown enough that it now looked more like a branch. The branch twisted, and more branches began sprouting from it, curving and bending into knots. What looked like eyes made of tree sap formed inside the branches and stared at Espen.

A head-shape began to form from the branches around the eye sockets. The eyes widened and moved apart, and a horse's long muzzle grew. Ears like his own sprouted from its head, made of leaves and wood. A mane of pine needles sprang up along a neck, stopping at a few inches long, identical to Espen's short, flat-shaved roached mane. A body began to form from the mass, pushing out from the back of the fake horse head.

Ever so slowly, Espen managed to get his legs working and backed up, away from the branch thing, until his back hit a bookshelf. His nostrils flared and his tail swished, knocking books from the shelves behind him. His instinct was to run, but the branch thing was on the table between him and the only way out.

A moment later, the twisting branches had settled into a shape. A horse identical to Espen now sat on the edge of the table. The mane, tail, and fur of the creature were made of pine needles. Its eyes were amber tree sap. The creature had even made a crude replica of Espen's school robes from bark. Espen and the creature were staring at each other in shock when the squirrel librarian appeared in the aisle behind the creature.

"What is this racket? This is a library! I'm going to have to ask you to—" The squirrel librarian's words cut off as the wooden Espen turned its head to look at her. Her mouth dropped open into a gasping O of surprise. With a chitter of fear, she turned tail and ran. Her long bushy tail waved like a flag of surrender as she fled back the way she'd come.

Espen's eyes widened. He began to call out after her, but the creature's form shuddered and the words died in his throat. The wood creaked softly as the long horse tail became bigger and bushier, and the long horse muzzle shrunk away, turning into the shorter, thinner squirrel muzzle. All traces of Espen were gone, and now the thing looked exactly like the squirrel librarian, down to the style of robes, height, and fur-length, albeit made entirely of bark and pine needles.

The wooden monster looked at him with its amber eyes and jumped down from the table. It crouched and then sprang towards Espen with claws outstretched and mouth open to show wicked looking incisors.

Fear made all the spells he'd been learning fly from his head, and muscle memory took over. Still clutching the book to his chest, Espen turned his torso and lifted a leg sideways. He snapped his leg out in a kick, and his hoof caught the wooden squirrel square in the chest. The creature flew backwards, landing on its back, but it used the momentum to roll under the table before springing to its feet on the other side. It turned around and made a very squirrel-like leap to the top of the closest bookshelf. Then it was gone, running away across the top of the shelves.

This was it. He was going to get kicked out. He couldn't go home; his parents had vehemently opposed him studying magic, and he'd had to run away in order to attend Dunwasser. He knew there was no way his parents would let him come back.

By the time Espen found the strength to move, the creature was long gone. He wandered the aisles for a few moments, trying to catch sight of it, but the spaces between the ceiling and the bookshelves was cast in shadow by the low table lamps. When he returned to the front lobby area, he realized he was still clutching the book about growing plants with magic. He ducked back behind a shelf, out of sight of the squirrel librarian who was frantically talking to a furred sumatran rhino professor. Espen stuffed the book in his school bag. He knew it was against the rules, but he needed to study the book and figure out what had gone wrong with his spell.

That done, he walked into the lobby. The squirrel's little ears still swiveled in his direction before he'd made four steps into the room. She turned to face him, pointing at him with an accusatory finger. Espen stopped, hanging his head with guilt.

"That's him," the librarian chittered.

The rhino delicately adjusted his glasses with his giant hands and peered at Espen through the thick lenses. "He looks fine to me, Professor Donnell."

"I'm telling you, I saw it." Professor Donnell crossed her arms and glared at Espen, her tail twitching erratically behind her. "It was him, but he'd turned himself into living wood." Espen glanced up, confused. Hadn't she seen him behind the wooden creature? Perhaps not. If all her attention had been on the plant monster, it would have been easy to miss his dull brown robes and fur in the shadows.

"I'm not saying you didn't see what you said you saw." The rhino leaned down to pat the much smaller squirrel's shoulder. "But from his robes, he *is* a student of earth magic. Maybe he was just practicing a spell?"

"Spell casting is forbidden in the library!" The squirrel rounded on the rhino, jamming her finger into his broad chest.

"We both know that students break that rule all the time." The rhino gently pushed the squirrel's arm away and then looked at Espen, giving him a sympathetic look. "It's fine, colt, you aren't in trouble." This did make Espen relax, at least fractionally. "You just scared Professor Donnell a little. Can you please explain what happened, to put her at ease?"

Espen thought fast and decided it would be best to just go along with the rhino. An unauthorized spell was one thing, but unleashing a monster in the school was a different story. Best not to mention it. Besides, the wood thing was probably long gone by now. "Ah, yes, I'm sorry. I didn't mean for my spell practice to frighten you, Professor Donnell. It won't happen again."

Professor Donnell glared at him, still suspicious, but Espen's apology seemed to satisfy the rhino, who nodded.

"There, see?" The rhino patted the squirrel's shoulder again. "I'm sure the colt learned his lesson."

"Humph." The squirrel rounded on Espen. "Fine. But I'll be keeping a very close eye on you from now on. Now, get out of my library. We're closed."

Espen nodded and trotted as fast as he dared out of the library, heading straight for his dorm room. He wished he'd tried to make friends with more of the other students so that he had someone to go to for help. But so many of them had given him a hard time about being a horse who wanted to be an Elementalist--one could only take so many jokes about not being able to punch through a written test--that he'd kept mostly to himself all semester.

It was dusk, and the hallways were almost empty. While there were classes for the nocturnal animals, they usually didn't start until later in the evening, and it was late enough that most of the diurnal animals had already left for home or their dorm rooms.

Espen turned down the hall that led to the student dorms and stopped dead in his tracks. The wooden squirrel was there, marching back and forth across the hall as if patrolling. In the dim twilight it looked almost like a real squirrel, except for the wood grain on its nose and its bright amber eyes.

Professor Donnell or the rhino professor would tell someone about the incident in the library. It would be easy to put two and two together if a student reported this creature. He had to get rid of it, before anyone else saw it.

Espen settled his school bag against his side and tightened the straps. If there was one benefit to being a horse, it was being able to run fast. He set his legs and took off at a running start, sprinting at the wooden creature. The wooden squirrel saw him and dashed away. Unfortunately, squirrels were no slouches in the speed department either. It darted back and forth, forcing Espen to continually read just his direction. Trying to keep footing on the slick floors was a challenge with hooves, and bit by bit, the wooden squirrel began to out pace him. But when it darted left, Espen knew he'd won. The doors down that hall were all kept locked. A dead end. He turned and slid on the slick wood, his hooves gouging the pristine hardwood floor.

The wooden squirrel was at the end of the hall, darting around and rattling locked door handles. Espen's hooves thundered as he charged towards the squirrel. He had it. The squirrel's unnatural amber eyes met his, and then it compressed, flattening itself out, and slithered—he had no other word for it, yet how could a plant slither?—through the thin gap between the door frame and the door at the far end of the hall. Espen was so startled that his legs lost the rhythm of the run, one hoof caught on his other leg and he went down in a tumble, crashing to the floor. His momentum rolled him into the door with a resounding thump that rattled the whole building. Doors popped open up and down the hall.

"What was that?" "Sounded like a whole herd of horses ran through." "I'm trying to sleep here!" and more shouts and jeers came at him as he crawled back to his hooves. Of course, one of the few doors that hadn't opened was the one he'd crashed into. The one he needed open.

One of the professors, a black fox who taught air magic, appeared at the end of the hall. "What's all this noise?"

"It's that horse who thinks he's a scholar," a golden retriever dog said from a doorway, turning to point at Espen. "He was running in the halls and slipped on the floor."

"Student Sverre, please come with me." The fox crossed his arms, looked pointedly down at the gouge in the floor before looking back up and giving Espen a withering glare.

Espen ducked his head, his ears splaying back in embarrassment. "Yes, professor."

Espen didn't get back to his room until much later. The professor had given him a very stern lecture about proper conduct while in the halls of the college and then given Espen a disciplinary slip. He was to wash dishes in the kitchen after class for the next week.

With a flick of his hand, Espen sent magic into the lamp next to his bed. The orb inside sprang to life, filling the room with yellow light. Luckily, he didn't have to worry about waking up a roommate. He'd been given a single room, since horses were significantly bigger than many of the other students.

Espen placed his school bag on the tiny desk while eyeing his bed with longing. He was exhausted and had class in the morning, but he needed to figure out what he'd accidentally revived.

Long hours of blurry-eyed reading later, he found his answer in a footnote attached to a word of warning.

"*While using magic to grow plants, be careful not to magically alter the plant itself[1].*"

At the bottom of the page, he found the footnote:

"*1. Look no farther than the infamous Pine Clone to see how disastrously wrong experiments like this can go.*"

A Pine Clone? He'd never heard of such a thing, but the name described his weird transforming pine twig perfectly. Espen sat back, tapping one hoof on the floor with a rhythmic clip-clop as he thought. He had a name for the creature, but now what? He sat forward and flipped through the book, rapidly scanning the pages, but didn't see Pine Clones mentioned anywhere else. He needed to go back to the library.

The square of his window was still totally dark. After closing for an hour at dusk, the library reopened for the nocturnal students. He'd never been there at night, but it was dark enough that it was probably still open.

Yawning, he repacked the stolen library book in his bag and headed off. The halls at night were filled with unfamiliar faces.

He was passing through a four-way intersection when he caught sight of a round, furry squirrel tail out of the corner of his eye down an otherwise empty hallway. He stopped and turned, recognizing Professor

Donnell's profile. She wouldn't be up at this hour, since she worked days in the library. It had to be his wooden squirrel, the Pine Clone!

Espen wanted to charge down the hall and catch it but his hooves pounding on the hardwood would give him away immediately and he already knew it was faster than him. He had a better idea. He pressed himself against a wall out of sight of the hallway and risked a peak around the corner. The squirrel was trudging down the walkway towards him. Its head was down, so he couldn't see the gold eyes. He couldn't make out details in the dim light of the infrequent lamps, but it was definitely Professor Donnell's shape. He crouched next to the door and waited.

"I've got you now," Espen growled and tackled it to the floor as soon as it came through the door. They landed hard, Espen on top, and the wooden squirrel let out a squeak. Espen also let out a snort of surprise at feeling soft fur beneath him instead of scratchy pine needles.

"Let me up, now!" a female chittered from underneath Espen's bulk.

Oh, no. Espen jumped to his hooves and was horrified to see the furious face of Professor Donnell turn to glare at him, her black eyes glinting with anger.

"Sorry, thought you were someone else," Espen stammered out and then turned and sprinted away. His ears went flat. He'd done it now.

He ducked through a side door into the gardens. A path wound through the lawn. Espen ignored it, taking advantage of the wide-open space. His hooves tore up huge divots in the dew-soaked dirt as he galloped as fast as he could towards the library. Running like this out in the open, the wind in his mane, he felt a little homesick for the wide, flat plains of the Avoirdupois lands.

His breath came out in thick white clouds in the coolness of the night air, and by the time he reached the library, he was covered in a white lather. He slowed to a trot and wiped the worst of it from his face and neck before opening the outer door and heading inside.

Espen took a moment in a nearby water closet to splash his face and catch his breath before entering the library. The doors were unlocked.

The sight inside felt slightly surreal, like he'd walked into another time and place. Despite the magically lit lamps burning cheerily on every table, without sunlight streaming in through the skylights the room was wreathed in shadow. A white rat with red eyes sat at the front desk in Professor Donnell's usual spot.

The rat hopped up from his chair and moved to intercept Espen as he crossed the lobby.

Espen stopped and turned to look down at him. "Are the daytime students not allowed to use the library at night?"

The rat held up a paw and wiggled it back and forth. "It's discouraged, but not really against the rules. We want to make sure our students are well rested. Mainly it comes up around exams or when a big paper is due, but I don't have anything like that showing on the schedule." He looked at Espen expectantly.

Espen shuffled his hooves and flicked his ears. "It's a little urgent. Well, I was here yesterday, or I guess earlier today? Anyway, I was reading 'Gardening with Magike' by Furaha Knaggs."

The rat's eyes widened. "Heavy reading for a first year student."

"It's a personal interest of mine. There was a magical plant mentioned in the book that I wanted to find out more about, a Pine Clone. Do you happen to know anything about it?"

The rat snorted with laughter. "That's what brought you to the library in the middle of the night?"

"It's kept me up all night." Espen shrugged. It was true, in a fashion. "I figured as long as I wasn't sleeping, I'd come to the library and see if I could find more out about it."

"Fair enough. Must have some burning curiosity to make you run all the way here." The rat nodded to the sweat stains on Espen's robes. "I'm Professor Geels. If you're this eager to learn about something not even in the curriculum, I'm sure I'll be seeing more of you around."

"Espen Sverre." Espen's ears went back and he ducked his head, but he held out his hand and shook the albino rat's outstretched paw.

"Right this way, I know just the book." Professor Geels led him through the library, talking the whole way. "Those plants are very interesting. Do you know we don't know where they originally came from? They aren't a natural plant. Scholars think they're a magician's experiment that escaped into the wild. They can copy almost any animal. Not exact, you know, but they can get eerily close."

"How dangerous are they?" Espen asked as Geels stopped at a bookshelf close to where the squirrel librarian had taken him.

Geels waggled his hand again. "Depends on their orders, but usually not." Espen frowned. That hadn't been his experience. Espen was about to ask more questions when a female voice came from behind them.

"Professor Geels, there you are. I need to know about Pine Clones, and--"

Espen turned, his heart dropping into his chest, as Professor Donnell came around the corner of a bookshelf. She stopped talking and stared back at Espen, seemingly as shocked to see him as he was to see her.

"You! What are you doing here?" they both said at the same time.

Geels was looking back and forth at both of them in confusion before bursting out laughing. "Two people confused about what the other one is doing there, asking about Pine Clones? Don't tell me, we have a clone loose on the campus."

Both he and Professor Donnell nodded.

"I'm sorry about tackling you earlier. I thought you were the clone," Espen admitted.

Professor Donnell gave him a sharp look. "We'll discuss that later. For now, we need to find that thing before it hurts anyone."

"How did you figure it out?" He'd seen the thing transform, the professor hadn't.

"At first I didn't," she admitted. "Then I remembered that stick you'd shown me and how that thing had looked just like you. I was on my way here to do more research when you tackled me, mistaking me for someone--or something--else, which confirmed my theory."

"So what do we do about it?" Espen asked, tensing up for what he knew was coming. "I understand

I'm going to be expelled, but I believe in cleaning up my own messes." Honor was everything for an Avoirdupois. Espen may have run away from his home and country, but he would always be an Avoirdupois at heart.

"As I said, we'll discuss your fate at this college later." She turned to Geels, who had been watching this exchange with his paws over his muzzle, not quite suppressing the fit of the giggles he was having. "Now, you were showing the colt books about the Pine Clone?"

"Yes, fascinating creature.," he said, and then repeated what he'd already told Espen. "This book has more information." He picked up a thick volume off a shelf and held it out to Professor Donnell.

"That will help later, but we don't have time for that now." The squirrel nervously chewed on a claw and then looked at Espen. "Where did you see it last?"

"In the dorms. I chased it down a hall and thought I had it, but it somehow crawled through a crack in door and I lost it."

"I take it that the clone looked like me at the time?"

Espen nodded.

"Won't stay that way, though," Professor Geels pipped up between giggles. "A wild one will change forms frequently."

Espen frowned and put a hand on his chin, thinking. "It's still a plant, right?"

Geels and Donnell both nodded.

"So it'll need sunlight, water, and soil at some point. Maybe we should start our search in the garden?"

"That's an idea." Professor Donnell nodded, her bushy tail twitching.

"Also," Espen's mind was churning now that the adrenaline was wearing off, "could we use the clone's magical signature to track it?" He couldn't remember where he'd read about that tidbit, but it made sense. Like the way scent-oriented species could follow a person's path using just their noses.

"We could," the rat spoke up now, his giggles almost gone. "But we'd need to be familiar with the traces of that particular magic. I haven't ever seen a Pine Clone in person." He turned to the squirrel, who shook her head.

"I'm familiar with it. . I'd had that sprig since I was a little colt, and I could feel magic emanating from it even then. It was my good luck charm," Espen said.

Professor Geels was already shaking his head. "Not going to work. That tracking spell is far too advanced for a first year student."

Professor Donnell gave Espen a thoughtful look. "I would have said that about the spells in the books I showed you earlier, Student Sverre. Yet, I'm taking it you cast 'Regrowth' and that accidentally revived the Pine Clone?"

Espen nodded, flicking one ear back in puzzlement. The squirrel almost sounded impressed.

"He can do it."

"Are you sure?" Professor Geels' black rat eyes were wide.

"I'm sure. Find the book with the spell and meet Espen and me in the garden." Professor Donnell turned to Espen, smiling so wide she showed her incisors. "Let's go."

The sun was just peeking above the horizon, streaking the sky with pinks and golds as Espen and Professor

Donnell entered the grassed commons outside of the garden. Dew still sparkled on the grass, steam rising as the sun began to burn it away. Fresh divots scarred the neatly-cut grass where Espen had run through just an hour earlier. The sight made him wince.

A fence enclosed the garden, and Professor Donnell stopped at the gate to survey the grounds. The garden was used for several classes. Espen had a beginning earth magics class here once a week, and he'd frequently seen another group of students at the other end tending to the plants and herbs, but he didn't know if it was for a class or just a hobby. This early in the morning the garden looked empty.

Since it was used for teaching, it was divided into sections that each featured plants from different climates and environments. There was a large clump of various pine trees towards the far end, and it was there at the professor seemed to focus her attention.

"Should we wait for Professor Geels?" Espen asked as Professor Donnell opened the gate and headed inside.

"Only if we can't find it visually." She glanced up at him as she spoke, and the bags under her eyes made her whole face look drawn. She looked as tired as he felt.

The squirrel trudged off down the path and Espen headed off in the opposite direction. "It'll be faster if we split up."

"Good idea. Call out if you find anything." The squirrel's bushy tail disappeared around a bend in the path, hidden from behind by a big bush with thick green leaves bigger than Espen's head.

It was slow going. Espen pushed aside branches and leaves, making sure he wouldn't miss the clone hidden under low-hung branches or in thick bushes.

After he'd been at it a while, Professor Geels found him and handed him a thick book. The rat's red eyes sparkled with excitement. "There you are. I found the spell. Page 109."

"Thanks." Espen settled down in the dirt cross-legged, spreading the book across his lap.

"I'm so excited to finally get to see a Pine Clone in person," Professor Geels said, sitting down next to Espen. His long, hairless pink tail wagged behind him, brushing the leaves around.

"They're pretty creepy," Espen said absentmindedly as he began studying the tracking spell. It actually looked easier than the spell he'd used to revive the clone.

Geels prattled on about magical creatures while Espen did his best to memorize the spell. Espen never responded, but that didn't seem to bother Geels.

Finally, Espen closed his eyes, held out his hand, concentrated on the feel of the clone's magic as he remembered it, and cast the spell. He felt the magic dancing around him, and then he felt a tug on the left side of his muzzle. When he opened his eyes, he could see a glowing blue line trailing through the garden to his left. The path the clone had taken!

"It worked," Espen said, shutting the book. Geels looked impressed. He stood up and took the book back from Espen's lap. But as soon as Espen moved to stand up the blue glow faded away.

"Lead the way." Professor Geels exclaimed.

"I can't." Espen hung his head. "The spell ended when I stood up."

"Oh, yeah. You'll need to concentrate on it to keep it going."

Espen groaned and sunk back down to the ground, holding back out his hand for the book. Opening back up to the page with the spell, he began casting it again. But he was exhausted, and the magic wavered again as soon as he moved. He opened his eyes after the third failed try to find Professor Geels poking his arm.

"Professor Donnell found it, come on," Geels said, taking back the book again.

Espen crawled back to his feet, yawning, and followed the white rat through the garden. A faint, "Over here!" reached his ears, and he was glad the rat had better hearing than him. He never would have heard the squirrel from this far away.

Professor Donnell waved at them from a bush as they came close. She was hiding behind the thicket, peering around it at something farther away. Espen and Geels tip-toed up and joined her.

Professor Geels gasped in surprise when he caught sight of the clone and Espen barely suppressed a groan. At some point it had taken the form of a tiger. In the bright sunlight, it was obvious that the thing was a plant, yet it was still eerie seeing a perfect copy of a tiger rendered in branches and pine needles. The clone was standing motionless in a big patch of ivy, facing towards the rising sun.

"What do we do now?" Espen whispered to the two professors.

Professor Donnell tapped one edge of her librarian's robe sleeve to show Espen the red fire symbols embroidered there. "It's a plant, so it should be afraid of fire. I'll circle around and drive it back to you, then you use your magic to move the earth out from underneath it. Trap it in a hole."

Espen nodded. "Got it." The spell to move earth was one of the first ones an Earth Elementalist learned. So far he'd only practiced with flinging things off tables, but moving the ground from underneath the Pine Clone's feet shouldn't be too different.

"What about me?" Professor Geels squeaked, his red eyes wide. He was clearly terrified.

"You run to get help if things go wrong."

Geels nodded.

Professor Donnell nodded back to him and crept away, keeping low to the ground. Slowly she made her way around the still clone. When she was in front of it, Espen lowered himself to a crouch and held out his hands, bringing the words of the spell to his mind. A small glowing golden ball appeared in his palms, ready to be thrown.

With a roaring battle-cry that impressed even Espen, Professor Donnell burst from the bushes directly in front of the clone. She held a ball of fire between her outstretched palms and she waved it at the wooden tiger.

The clone stumbled backwards, and Espen tossed the golden ball of his earth magic. It hit the ground at the wooden tiger's feet and earth exploded up around it in a plume. The squirrel had been too close, and the earth plume hit her arms, knocking her backwards. She flailed, trying to keep her balance, and accidentally let go of the glowing ball of fire. It flew into the cloud of dust flying around the clone, whooshing as it hit something inside. Chunks of earth, plants, and rock began to rain down around them. Geels squealed and ducked, holding the library book above his head. Espen lifted his arm and covered his face, trying to keep the flying debris out of his eyes.

A moment later the deluge stopped and Espen dropped his arm, waving his hand in front of his nose to clear some of the dust away. He peered through the cloud, catching sight of a bright yellow glow.

The good news was his spell had worked perfectly. The clone was at the bottom of a hole about three paces around. The bad news was that it was only about three hands deep. Espen estimated that if he stood in it, it would only come up to his knees.

The even worse news was that the clone was on fire. It ran around the shallow hole, its pine needle fur burning merrily. Stopping, the clone shook its limbs to dislodge the burning needles. They went out as they fell into the dirt, leaving singed and smoldering branches bare.

Professor Donnell, hacking and coughing, was just getting to her feet on the other side of the hole. Being so close, she'd been hit with the worst of the debris. Her robes and fur were so covered in dirt that she looked made out of earth.

Her coughing drew the clones attention, and it turned its back on Espen, moving towards the squirrel. The professor's eyes were glued shut with the dust, so she couldn't see the danger.

"No!" Espen shouted, bursting from his hiding place behind the thicket. The wooden tiger had crouched with claws bared and was about to leap at the helpless squirrel. Espen charged, jumping at the edge of the shallow hole to tackle the clone from behind. They went down in a heap, landing with the clone face down on the ground underneath Espen. In the tiger shape, the clone was almost as big as him.

The clone's limbs were still hot from the fire, burning Espen's skin where it wasn't protected by his school robes. The Pine Clone bucked and writhed under him, swiping at him with wooden tiger claws. Espen tried to hold on and pin the clone's arms, but it was just too strong.

163

The fight was strangely silent except for Espen's grunts as wrestled with the clone. For its part, the clone didn't make a sound. The wooden tiger made an undulating motion with its back and cracked the end of Espen's muzzle with the back of its head. Blood gushed from Espen's nose as he reared back and let go of the thing's arms. The clone twisted under him, slashing at his exposed chest with its wooden claws.

Blood welled from the cuts, and the pain was excruciating, like three lines of fire burning down his front. Espen's scream was echoed by Professor Geels. The rat turned on his heels and dashed away, screaming for help. Ignoring the pain in his chest and nose, Espen made a fist and punched the wooden tiger's face. The clone's head snapped back and Espen grabbed the clone's wrists and pushed them to the ground. They struggled against each other. Professor Donnell recovered and lifted her hands to do a spell but hesitated, clearly unsure how to blast the clone without hitting Espen as well.

His vision had narrowed to a pin prick by the time he heard a commotion to the side and heard Professor Geels yelling, "Over here!" Suddenly they were surrounded by mages. Someone cast a spell and the clone went limp. With the resistance gone, Espen collapsed on top of it.

"Is that blood?" "Get a healer!" "Stay steady." Everyone was yelling at once around him.

Espen crawled off the clone and lay back in the grass, as far away from the chaos as he could get. As soon as he moved, a group of excited mages and scholars circled the still Pine Clone, chattering loudly.

An armadillo in the robes of a healer came up to him.

"May I heal your wounds, noble steed?" she asked quietly, kneeling at his side.

Espen nodded and the armadillo monk held her hands over his lacerated chest. A moment later energy flooded through him, washing away the pain. The cuts scabbed over and by the time she pulled her hands away, it looked like they were weeks old. Not the battle scars his father had expected him to get, but still Espen was proud of them.

"Thank you." Espen said. The armadillo looked pleased, giving him a small bow before getting to her feet and wandering off to check that no one else needed her services.

Espen got up, intending to go back to his dorm and pack. He needed to figure out what to do with his life now that his dream of being a mage was shattered.

Professor Donnell ran up to him as he began to walk away. "Where are you going, Student Sverre?"

"To get my things..." he trailed off as she glared at him, her bushy tail snapping irritably.

"What makes you think you're expelled?"

Espen merely waved a hand to the chaos going on around the fallen Pine Clone.

The squirrel shook her head. "You made a mistake. Students do. But you did your best to try to clean up your mess, even though you should have asked for help sooner. I trust you've learned your lesson about swallowing your pride, and asking for help when you need it?"

Espen nodded vigorously. "Yes, professor."

Professor Donnell smiled. "I thought so. A hard lesson, but a good one to learn early. "

"What will happen to the clone?" Espen looked back at the chaos, still curious about the strange magical plant despite everything.

"It's the perfect opportunity for the students to be able to study a rare plant," the squirrel gave a wry smile. "The hardest part will be getting the thing to stay put."

Espen laughed.

The White Deer

This story was originally published in Zooscape Magazine edited by Mary E. Lowd in the December 2020 edition.

Fairies can kiss my white-tailed ass. I never liked fairytales, even before I found out that fairies were the ones responsible for my "condition." As soon as I was old enough to talk, I peppered my parents with questions about why I couldn't go play outside like the other children. At first my mom placated me with vague platitudes of "when you're older" but eventually the truth came out.

I've been cursed by a fairy. No really. There was even a video of the fateful event. My mom let me watch it after finally letting it slip one day. I think it was after watching one of those Disney movies where the fairies were helpful and kind.

The video was taken at my first birthday party. My parents had invited anyone and everyone who was anyone. All the famous celebrities had vied to attend. My dad's a successful movie star. Well, my mom too.

They both had been made famous in the same debut, playing the Prince and Princess on a mega-famous TV show. It had been the talk of the tabloids when they ended up getting married for real. When I came along the media dubbed me Princess. The nickname stuck.

Anyways, my parents turned my first party into quite the event of the season. Everybody brought gifts. You can see them, piled in the corner of the video. Jewelry, perfume, statues, stuffed animals, and more. Lots of stuff inappropriate for a baby, if you ask me.

At first, the video focuses on me. The view pans around to the room as a woman sweeps in all dramatic like. She's older, in a layered red dress with poofy skirts that fall all the way to the floor. A mask shaped like a crab covers her face except for her eyes. Still, you can tell her age by the tight-highness of her voice, the wrinkles and age spots on her hands, and the slate-gray of her hair that's pulled into an intricate bun on the top of her head.

She rants about not being invited to her own god-daughter's birthday party. The overhead lights begin flickering on and off as the woman storms across the room. You could tell the person behind the camera is terrified, the way it bounces all over. You can even hear his muttered cursing in the background. Still, my parents hired a professional. He keeps filming.

The woman gets to me where I'm sitting up in a high chair, birthday cake smeared all over my face and hands. My mother throws herself between me and the woman. "I'm sorry I forgot to invite you. I made a terrible mistake. Please don't take it out on my baby."

Then come the fateful lines. "Very well." Her back is to the camera now, but you can hear the sneer in her voice. "I'll let the child live. After all, my magic worked so hard to help you create her. Still, there must be a price to be paid. If she sees sunlight before she is married, a terrible fate will befall her."

My mother falls to her knees, crying, as the woman in red laughs. In the flickering lights, it's hard to tell, but it looks like her form withers and shrinks until she vanishes altogether. If you play the video frame-by-frame, there was a brief point, a single frame long, where I'd swear she was a crab. But my mother disagrees.

That was the end of the video. Or at least the part my mom showed me. But I could hear the way, before my mom turned it off, that the guests started to laugh as the lights come back on. They probably thought it was a prank. But my mom knew better.

This next part, the why, I didn't get till a few years later. We were in the kitchen of our underground house – no sunlight remember –cooking dinner. Well, mostly I was cooking under my mom's instruction, as she slowly finished off a bottle of wine. My mom got drunk, and admitted that after trying and failing to have a child, they tried fertility treatments. They'd sunk millions in that, with no success. At least until they tried some "alternative" treatments involving a mushroom fairy ring and a summoning spell. She confessed that they'd both been very high and not a little drunk. Apparently it had been uproariously funny when they dreamed that a self-proclaimed fairy had actually answered their summons. Quite the hallucination! Especially the way her form wavered from crab to woman and back again inside the circle of mushrooms.

She thought it a coincidence when nine months later I was born. But then, at the party, it all came back to her and she knew it hadn't been a dream. My father thought it was nonsense, but my mother believed in the curse.

At least I had the Internet. I took all my classes online, and my tutors Skyped in if they couldn't come in person. It did get a little lonely. When I watched TV shows where the classrooms are filled with kids my age, I couldn't help but feel a little bit jealous. It wasn't like I never saw anyone in person. Mom and Dad continued to do movies, and I got to go to quite a few of the release parties, since they usually didn't start until after dark anyway. And sometimes my parents would throw parties at our house, in the regular, upstairs part. The underground part was our little secret, since no one else believed my mom about the curse.

In my spare time, I read every bit of lore, legend, and tale about fairies I could find, looking for a way out.

I had lots of friends online, and I debated with them about what to do. I needed to get married to break the curse, but, ugh, marriage. Once I hit sixteen, Dad started bringing home some of his teenage costars. Frankly, I really did not see what all the fuss was about. I never really had much in common with them, and they were almost never as cute in person as they were on the TV screen.

My Internet friends would always gasp and wail when I'd tell them this after the parties. "How can you say that about Joshua?" Or "Freddie?" Or whoever the hot new guy was that week.

"I'm just not that into them," I'd frequently say with a shrug. "Anyway, if I had my wish it would be to meet any of you in person."

This particular day I was video chatting with Zach. Zach was my best friend, and the one that I really longed to meet in person. She hated her birth name, so she was trying out the name Zach right now.

I lay on my stomach on my bed, head in my hands, laptop set in front of me. Zach was at her computer desk, movie posters plastered the wall behind her head. She leaned back in her chair and put her hands behind her head as she listened to me telling her about last night's party, and the boy my parents had shoved at me. A boy who's smiling face stared at me mockingly from one of the posters behind Zach.

"Honestly, Princess," Zach shoved her keyboard away so she could put her elbows on the desk and her head in her hands, mimicking my pose. "Just pick one and marry him. You can always get divorced after the curse is broken."

I don't think Zach believed me about the curse. She played along, but the flippant way she talked about it told me she wasn't taking me seriously. I groaned and flopped face first onto the covers. "That feels like a copout. Besides, I'm seventeen. Too young to get married. And especially not to movie star. It's like you've never read a tabloid before."

"You know," Zach sounded thoughtful. "My school is doing a trip to San Francisco next week to attend the high school national shooting competition. Maybe we can meet up in person while I'm there."

I glanced up to see the screen, expecting Zach to stick out her tongue at me or something, so I'd know she's joking. Instead, to my surprise, she looked serious. I blinked at her image on my laptop screen for a few minutes. "You realize LA is in Southern California right? Not anywhere near San Francisco."

"It can't be that far."

I sat up and shifted to sit cross legged in front of my laptop. "This isn't like your tiny Eastern states." Not like I'd ever been, but we liked to tease each other. "That's like an all day drive up there with traffic."

Not that I'd ever been. But my parents had and were always complaining about the traffic. Zach pouted at me and I sighed. She was right though. This was probably our best chance. "All right, all right. I'll talk to my mom."

The next morning at breakfast, I was eating cereal at the island in the underground kitchen when my mom came in. Now or never. "Hey Mom."

"Yes, Princess?" She opened the fridge and began rummaging through. "I'm listening."

"One of my Internet friends is coming on a trip to San Francisco next week." I could practically hear my mom's frown, even with her back turned me so I rushed through the rest of my proposal. "I want to go up there to meet them."

My mom emerged from the fridge with her arms full of supplies to make breakfast, and shut the door with the kick of her leg. She dumped everything on the counter next to the stove and got out a pan before answering. "You know that's not possible. Why not have your friend come to you?"

"It's a school trip. They can't leave the group."

My mom shook her head and cracked an egg into the pan. "Absolutely not. It's too dangerous until you get married and break the curse. And you've shot down every guy we introduced you to."

"But I'm so excited to meet Zach in person —"

My mom dropped the spatula—startling me so I stopped talking—and turned to stare at me. "Zach? Are you showing interest in a boy?"

I knew it was wrong, but I saw my opening. I bit my lip and blushed. It wasn't entirely an act. "I am very interested in Zach, yes."

My mom's eyes blazed and she clapped her hands. "Wonderful! I'll call ahead and set up reservations at a restaurant on the waterfront. Alioto's will stay open late if I ask."

"Aren't we both a bit young for marriage? We're both still high schoolers, after all." I don't know what my mom was thinking. I knew I already had her hook line and sinker, but it'd look suspicious if I didn't put up a token protest.

My mom waved this way with an airy wave of her hand. "Not at all. You meet, and if you like each other I'm sure we can arrange an emergency ceremony that very night."

My eyes went wide. The train was already getting out of control. "But Zach's parents—"

"If you do decide to go through with it I'll fly them out. I'm sure they'll understand if I talk to them on the phone." My mom rushed out of the room, in her excitement leaving the egg to burn in the pan on the stove.

"I'm sure they'll be so star struck at finding out who you are that you'll be able to get away with it, yes," I muttered to the empty kitchen as I went over and turned off the burner.

Zach was so excited when I told her that night. "I can't believe I get to meet you!"

"My mom's even getting us reservations at Alioto's for that night." I told her, still in amazement that my mom had agreed to this. "One hitch though. She thinks you're a guy."

Zach doubled over laughing and pulled her shoulder-length hair back behind her head with one hand. "How you doing?" she said with an exaggerated deep voice and pointed at the laptop camera. Then she winked at me. I laughed.

"But seriously," I said, wiping the tears of mirth from my eyes with my sleeve. "What are we going to do?"

"I'll think of something." She grinned at me, bouncing up and down on her chair in excitement. "There's been something I've been aching to try, and this is the perfect excuse."

"I wish I could go with you, dear," my mom said, kissing me on each cheek. The sun had not yet risen, and the chilled morning air made me shiver in my thin shirt. My mom and dad both had movie shoots today, so I was being driven alone to San Francisco by a hired driver. My mom had gotten a special window tinting treatment done on one of her cars so that I could ride in the backseat without seeing sunlight.

"I'm sure I'll be fine." I assured her. "I'll call you from the restaurant once I get there."

"Please do that." My mom said and then turned to my driver, Madeleine. "You keep my little girl safe, you hear me?"

Madeleine nodded, looking serious. She was attending dinner with Zach and I as a chaperone. I told Zach last night by phone, and she had assured me again that she had it all taken care of.

"I will, ma'am."

My mother gave Madeleine a sharp nod and headed for the car idling at the curb that would take her to her movie shoot. We both waved as she pulled away and then Madeleine ushered me towards my specially outfitted car that was sitting in the driveway. I climbed in the back seat, and Madeleine in the front. She put the key in the ignition and pressed a button. The divide between the front and back seats whirred slowly closed, encasing me in darkness. I quickly turned on the overhead light. I shivered as I felt the car rock as Madeleine backed down the driveway and out onto the street.

The rocking motion of the car on asphalt combined with the inability to look at the windows left me motion sick. Occasionally I used the intercom to message Madeleine and get updates on where we were, since I couldn't see the street signs. After what felt like an eternity, Madeleine told me, "About forty more minutes. We just passed through San Jose, and are currently driving through the hills outside San Francisco."

"Is it dark yet? I really need to get out and stretch my legs." And use the bathroom, but I didn't need to tell her that.

"Sorry, Princess. In fact, at this rate we'll get to San Francisco before dark."

I took my hand off the intercom button, and sat back with a sigh, going back to watching a movie on my iPad. Unexpectedly, I felt the car slow.

The intercom crackled on, and Madeleine's voice came through. "Got off at a rest stop. Your question made me realize I need a break, and since we're ahead of schedule I know you won't mind."

I huffed. Madeleine had a point. But I felt petty enough that I didn't reply. A moment later the car rocked as Madeleine's door opened and she got out. I was jealous as I imagined her walking through the sunshine. I'd seen it so many times in the movies that I could visualize what it looked like.

However, Zach had described to me about the warmth of the sun and how it felt tingly on your skin after a long day indoors. Movies couldn't simulate that. Maybe Zach was right that I should just get married to the next guy my parents pushed at me. Not like I hadn't thought about it before. Quick marriage. Quicker divorce. But ever since I found out I was cursed, I'd done a lot of reading about fairies. Everything I read suggested that they were quite literal, and if the curse meant I had to be married for the curse to be broken, if I got divorced it might come back since then I would no longer be married.

I shook my head. All this was speculation anyway. The intercom crackled to life, and I jumped in surprise. I hadn't heard the driver's door open, or felt the car shift like Madeleine had returned.

A voice came through the intercom, along with deep breathing. There was a lot of static too, and I leaned closer to hear better. I could almost make out words, as if a heavy breather was sub vocalizing or whispering them. Then to my horror, I heard the whir of a window going down to my left. I scrambled away, huddling down in the footwell, but I couldn't avoid the piercing rays of light in the small backseat of the car. After a moment there was another whir as the passenger side window and the partition with the front seat both began lowering. There was nowhere I could go.

I cringed as the first light hit my face. Where the light hit fur began sprouting up, and I screamed at the sensation of it prickling out through my skin. I thrashed and writhed, hitting the door with my back. It opened, or rather someone opened it, and I spilled out onto the asphalt, landing on my back. Looking down at me was Madeleine's shocked face. I cried and begged for help, but my words came out garbled as my mouth transformed like the rest of me. I held out my hands to her for help, only to see my fingers fuse together and turn brown and hard.

I could feel my legs shifting as well and heard a thump as my shoes fell off. I rolled over onto my stomach and stood up to all fours, balancing on long slender legs and arms now tipped with hooves. I raised my head, flicking my now large ears that stuck out from my head, and then turned my head to look down the length of myself.

I was now a deer, with snow white fur poking out from beneath my jeans and T-shirt. My legs felt constricted in the rough fabric of my jeans. They were already half fallen off, so I pranced about with a little kick of my back legs that threw off the jeans, stumbling as I got used to the way my new legs worked.

Experimentally I flipped my puff of a tail, and it bobbed about on command.

Nothing hurt, and satisfied that all my pieces were there and accounted for, I looked about myself. We were at a rest stop off the highway. There were a few other cars parked in the lot, and a growing crowd of people wandering my way, pulling out cameras to point at me. All I could see, besides the rest stop and the highway, were brown hills full of dry grass and trees.

I felt a sudden urge to get away from the large press of people. Hooves clattering on asphalt, I stumbled away into the brush. Walking with all four legs was complicated, and at first I had to walk in a stiff-legged gait as I concentrated on getting all four of my limbs to move in concert. A while longer and I was bounding along like I'd been born a deer. Now that I had figured out walking, I was able to properly stop and appreciate the sunlight beating down on me. Zach had been right about how warm it was.

Zach. I vaguely remembered her face, but the longer I was a deer, the more I felt like a deer. I caught myself grazing on the dry leaves as I walked more than once. I began to wonder about the cloth around my neck and front half and why it was there. It kept catching on the sun-dried twigs of the trees I moved through. I tried to keep moving north, despite not being able to remember why. The farther north I went, the more houses I spotted. I was drawn to them, but my deer nature was skittish of the humans that moved around those dwellings, and so I avoided them.

As twilight fell, my limbs began to tingle. I found a large evergreen with low branches and crawled underneath, laying down and tucking my long hooved legs underneath me. The reverse of the transformation was slower, but just as painful. Once I was fully human again I lay on the bed of soft pine needles and hugged myself, shivering. I was naked except for the torn remains of my T-shirt.

This was not good. Given my "condition" I'd never been camping or spent really any time at all in the outdoors. I didn't even have my phone or any way to call for help, since that had been in the pocket of my jeans, which my deer-self had kicked off in a panic. At least I wasn't hungry. As a deer I'd been grazing on the foliage all day as I walked.

As I lay there trying to think of what to do, I heard a scuttling on pine needles, and sat up in alarm. The sky was the deep purple of twilight, and the light had not yet faded entirely. I squinted my eyes against the gloom, trying to see what was disturbing the dried pine needles. I blinked as a crab crawled into view, the dull brown of its carapace blending in with the dark pine needles. The crab crawled closer, clacking its pincers at me. I scrambled backwards.

The edges of the crab began sparkling and soon the crab's entire body was engulfed in a blue light. The light brightened and expanded, and when it faded, a woman in a red dress stood there, hunched over, under the bows of the tree. The woman from the videos. The crab mask was pushed high on her head so I could see her face.

"Well, girl," the woman—the fairy—said, looking down her nose at me. "Your parents thought they could escape the consequences of their actions, but I knew if I was patient that eventually I would see justice done. So lucky that the electrical system of the car shorted out like it did." She winked at me.

"Justice?" I sputtered, angrily getting to my feet. I kept my hands clasped across my chest in a vague attempt to keep my tattered shirt from showing everything. "How is this justice?" I stomped my foot. "I've done nothing to wrong you."

The fairy shrugged, and twirled, I could see that her feet under her red dress as it lifted were not human feet but crab legs. "Wrong me? No. But your parents never came through on their end of the bargain, and so your life is mine to do with as I wish. Come serve me in my castle for seven years, and in return I'll see the curse lifted."

Seven years? That felt like an eternity. And what would happen to Zach, and my parents, while I was gone? I glared at the fairy in defiance. Not to mention knowing what I knew about fairies, I knew there had to be a catch. "No."

The fairy clacked angrily, and I looked at her hands to see that they had turned back into claws which were rapidly clacking open and closed. "Fine then. Another week as a deer should soften you up." And with that she disappeared in a sparkling twinkle of light.

Shivering, I lay back down and cried myself to sleep.

A crack of gunfire shattering the morning brought me fully awake. The sun had already risen and I'd changed back into a deer as I slept. Gunfire meant people, and people meant help. Shooting also reminded me of Zach and her competition. The deer part of me wanted to run from the sound, but today I was able to hold onto myself more, overcome my instincts, and force myself towards the sound.

I bounded quickly through the forest on my four legs, following the narrow game trails other deer had carved through the forest. The sounds of gunfire grew louder as I crested the hill. Below me was a shooting range set into the base of the hill. I moved out onto a rise so I could look down at the humans below me. My tail flicked up as I stared down at the group with my sensitive ears pinned to my head in a futile attempt to lessen the crack of the gunfire.

I felt drawn to the little people milling below, though I couldn't say why. I backed off the rise and wound my way down the hill, pushing through the brush. Not surprisingly, none of the game trails came close to the shooting range.

A tall fence encircled the property. I could maybe have jumped over it, but I was still not entirely used to my four-legged form. Besides, I didn't want to accidentally get shot. I pushed out of the brush and came into a parking lot. Several buses were in the lot, each one had the banner of a different school on it. As I looked towards the door, a group of teenagers spilled out. They were led by none other than Zach. I recognized her immediately, even with her hair cut short and her chest bound flat.

The teenagers all piled to a stop, gasping and pointing at me. The sun beat down on me from high in the sky, and my deer nature screamed at me to run. But Zach's staring face drew me to her. Walking slowly, each step was a slow fight against my deer instincts.

Zach was so handsome. Better looking in person even than she had been over video chat. I walked up until we were nose to nose.

Zach stared into my eyes, her eyes wide, her breathing fast and hard. "Princess?" she whispered.

I bobbed my head. Zach reached up to touch me when a door slammed, startling me. I jumped sideways and back, and my deer instincts took over, driving me out of the parking lot and away from the humans.

"Wait!" I heard Zach call out behind me, but it was too late; I couldn't stop myself from bolting.

A rifle barked and a piercing pain shot up my flank and down one of my back legs. I stumbled, but was able to keep going despite the pain. I staggered, limping my way back into the dry woods outside the shooting range.

"Don't shoot her!" Zach yelled.

I heard a human stumbling through the woods behind me, which only heightened my terror. I kept going; the sharp copper tang of my blood filled my nose, leaving a trail behind me that the more rational part of myself knew would draw predators to me.

Eventually I collapsed, folding my hooves under me, unable to go any farther. My injured back leg, where I'd been shot, I stuck out to the side. I closed my eyes and panted.

The sun was low when Zach came stumbling up behind me, filthy and sweating in the summer California heat and carrying a compact plastic first aid kit in one hand. She fell to the ground next to me and opened up the kit.

I looked at her dully, the pain making it hard to think. Zach held out a hand towards me, and I craned my neck out to sniff it.

"Princess—" Zach smiled, and I allowed her to pet my nose. "Can I bandage you up?"

I flicked my tail and one ear in amusement and bobbed my head at her. I looked back at her while she worked on my injured leg. My white fur was stained with blood in a trail all the way down to my hoof.

"You're probably wondering about my outfit," she said as she worked. I appreciated the distraction of conversation, wincing as she rubbed an alcohol wipe along where the bullet had grazed my left flank. She glanced up at me and smiled, making my heart skip a beat. I flicked my ears and nuzzled her side with my muzzle. She giggled and rubbed me between the ears with her free hand. Then she tugged at her shirt and touched her short hair by her ears. "I dressed as a guy so we could fool your mom. I gotta say though, I really love it!" She giggled and went back to dressing my wound. "I'm using he pronouns now. And I think I want to transition."

As Zach was taping on the last of the dressing, the sun went down the rest of the way. Zach gasped and fell back as my fur began to shimmer and I transformed. A moment later I lay there as a human again, flexing my fingers to get used to the feel of them after having hooves all day.

"Princess, it really is you!" Zach pulled me into a hug. I hugged her, or him now, back.

"It is." As much as I would have loved to hug Zach forever, I pushed him back so I could look at him. "How did you know?"

Zach smiled and touched my check. "I'd know those lovely eyes anywhere." Zach let his hand trail lower, to the last scraps of the shirt that hung off my shoulders. "Plus, I recognized your shirt. I've mentioned it being my favorite one of yours. And when I called your phone after you didn't show up for dinner the other night, your driver told me a wild tale about you turning into a snow white deer."

I bit my lip and nodded, unable to stop the tears that sprung up. "It's the curse, Zach." I told him about my visit from the fairy and her offer of servitude to take away the curse.

He took off his shirt while I talked and offered it to me. Underneath he wore a second shirt that looked stretchy and flattened his chest. I took the shirt gratefully, tearing off the last of my rags before pulling it over my head.

"What am I going to do, Zach?" I asked, rubbing my injured thigh. The bandage itched on my skin.

"I know seven years seems like forever, but you'd only be twenty-three or twenty-four by the time you serve out your sentence. I could wait for you." He took my hand and kissed it.

I shook my head. "I don't trust the fairies. Haven't you ever read any of the old tales?"

Zach shook his head.

"In almost all the stories, time in fairyland passes differently than in the real world. Seven years there could be seventy, or seven-hundred years back here."

Zach's eyes widened. "Oh." He frowned. "So, you turn into a deer only during the day."

I nodded my head and touched the bandage on my leg. "That guy tried to shoot me. Why?"

He tapped the breast of the shirt I now wore and scowled. I pulled it out so I could see the logo. It was hard as it was getting darker, but I made out a pair of crossed rifles. "He shouldn't have done that. It's not hunting season. I was in a hurry to get the first aid kit and go after you or I would have yelled at him. At least I heard the teacher reaming him out as I was leaving."

"What are we going to do now?" I shivered and hugged Zach closer. "I'm going to turn into a deer again tomorrow. What if there are other hunters around?"

"Come back to the hotel with me." Zach cuddled me protectively. "You can stay there during the day, at least for the next few days."

I shook my head. "I can't stay locked in a hotel room all day. When I'm a deer, I feel like a deer. I don't know if I could keep from destroying the room in a panic to get out."

"Shit." Zach sighed. "Well, can you meet me here tomorrow at dusk? I'll bring you clothes and try to come up with a better plan."

I bit my lip. "What if hunters shoot at me again?"

"They shouldn't. It's not hunting season. But..." Zach trailed off as I stiffened and touched my leg. "Your white color does stand out." He mused. He let me go and scooted back from me to take a handkerchief from the front pocket of his jeans. He carefully folded it up into a triangle and took both ends. "Here." He got on his knees and leaned towards me, wrapping the cloth around my neck and knotting it at the base of my throat. "The cloth collar should give people pause, at least. I'll bring a proper collar for you tomorrow. We can say you're my pet when you are in deer form."

It was dark enough now I couldn't quite see the gift properly, but I smiled and reached up to touch the cloth. Zach leaned over me and brought his lips to mine gently for a moment, then sat back.

"You be okay alone until tomorrow night?" he asked softly.

I smiled, although I knew he probably couldn't see me in the dark. "I will be now."

I found a safe spot to sleep under a tree and managed to wake up before the sun rose the next morning, in time to take off my shirt before transforming into a deer, but I left on the crude collar. My leg hurt, but not bad. I spent the day bounding about the hills outside San Francisco, munching on the leaves and grass.

As we planned I returned back to the area near the shooting range as it began to get dark. I found Zach pacing nervously near the spot where I met him yesterday. He wore an outfit similar to the day before, and a bulging backpack sat at his feet.

His eyes went wide as I pranced towards him in my deer form. He hardly dared breathe as I came up to him and nuzzled his shoulder with my muzzle. I was still a bit skittish as he petted me, but as a deer I was more comfortable around him than the day before. He stood with me until the sun went down and I fell to the dirt, my hooves splitting into fingers and my fur withdrawing back into my skin.

He helped me sit up, and retrieved a bottle of water from his backpack which he helped me sip from for a moment before offering me a pile of clean, folded clothes.

"So what's the plan?" I asked him breathlessly as I got dressed. I pulled the shirt on first, then sat down and put on the pants. Before I stood up he offered me a pair of flip-flops.

"I didn't know your shoe size and I forgot to ask yesterday, sorry," he said as I stood and slipped my feet through the flip-flop straps. They were a little big, but serviceable. "Come with me," he said, taking my hand. We began to move down the trail, down the hill towards the shooting range. "I've been thinking about the curse and how to break it."

"We can't," I said. "I'd have to get married to break the curse."

It was light enough I could still see the smile on his face. "I know, that's the idea." He wouldn't say anymore, no matter how much I pressed him as we hiked down the hill. We came to the blacktop and turned, following the curve of the road down into the parking lot of the shooting range. There was only one bus remaining in the parking lot, with a gaggle of bored teenagers hanging around outside it. They looked up at our approach, as if expecting us.

One of them stepped out of the group and approached us, a dark-haired girl with glasses. I had seen her pictures before on Zach's Facebook page. His friend Emily.

"Everything's ready inside," she said to Zach before turning to me and thrusting her hand out. "Hi, you must be Princess. I'm Emily."

Zach paused long enough for me to shake her hand. "Nice to meet you. What, exactly, is going on?"

"Inside, you'll see!" she said with a big smile, dashing ahead of us to open the door to the shooting range's shack.

Inside had been decorated with white streamers and balloons. A grocery store cake decorated with white frosting sat on a glass counter filled with guns and ammunition. Two adults, a man and a woman, wearing an outfit almost identical to Zach's stood inside, along with a portly man who wore a green polo shirt with the shooting range's logo on it.

They all introduced themselves to me, but I was so overwhelmed that I blanked on all their names. The woman flourished an official looking piece of paper at us.

"I am now officially licensed to perform weddings in the state of California!" she announced proudly. All pieces fell into place. I squealed and whirled around to hug Zach. He hugged me back tightly. Then he let go and dropped to one knee in front of me, pulling a little ring box out of his pocket and presenting it to me.

"I know it's sudden, and we're young, but will you marry me, Bright Heart?" he blurted out, his voice shaking. I winced at his use of my official name. There were many reasons I preferred the nickname Princess, the main one being my official name was stupid. That's what you get with movie star parents who did a lot of drugs when you were younger. That, and evil fairy godmothers. All in all, I could've done without either one.

I wiped the tears from my eyes, and fell to my knees in front of him and wrapped my arms around his shoulders. "Yes," I whispered into his ear around the lump that formed in my throat.

Crying, he hugged me back, the ring box digging into my back. The ceremony was short but sweet. The teacher led the ceremony, and we both said our "I do's" before Zach slipped the cheap plastic ring on my finger, and then we kissed while everyone clapped. Pieces of the grocery store cake were passed out on paper plates. Then we all trooped out to the bus. I didn't let go of Zach's hand the whole time.

Zach and I sat next to each other on the bus, I rested my head on Zach's shoulder and admired the ring on my finger in the light of the passing cars. It was ugly, but it was mine and I loved it. "Don't we need our parent's permission to get married?" I said softly, hoping the ceremony had been enough to break the fairy's curse.

"Nope," Zach laughed softly. "Not at seventeen."

The bus dropped us off in front of a hotel, and we all retired to our rooms for the night. I called my mom from Zach's room, and told her where I was. Of course she'd believed Madeleine when she'd been told about my transformation, and had had searchers out looking for me near the rest stop. But they hadn't realized I'd gone so far north. My mom wanted to drive over right then, but I was so tired. We told her we'd see her in the morning, and then we both went to bed. Zach spooned me and it felt right. I never wanted anyone or anything else.

I guess I figured that'd be the end of it. But no. I woke up the next morning in the throes of transformation. Suddenly, Zach had to deal with sharing a bed with a very large and very confused white doe. There was a lot of shouting, mostly from Zach, and bleats of terror, mostly from me.

I sprinted around the room that was suddenly far too small for my long, gangly legs. Zach managed to herd me into the bathroom, cornering me, and grabbed my head, petting me between the ears and whispering soothing words until I settled down and stopped kicking.

I rolled my eyes at him, still terrified. I hadn't been prepared for the transformation, and my deer instincts had taken over completely. But the smell of him combined with his soft talking eventually calmed me down.

I lay with my head resting in his lap. He slumped exhausted over the side of the bathtub. He looked at me, his hair rumpled from sleep and his eyes filled with tears. "It didn't work..."

A clacking sound in the bathtub caught both our attention. A crab crawled up the side of the bathtub to perch on the edge. A human voice came from crab's mouth as it scuttled back and forth by Zach's head.

"Of course it didn't work, deary," the crab said in the fairy's high-pitched voice. The crab cackled and clicked its claws. "You had to have been married before seeing sunlight the first time."

Being a deer I couldn't talk, but Zach asked her the question I was thinking. "So she'll be like this for the rest of her life? Only human at night?"

The crab scuttled close to Zach's face and snapped a claw at his nose. He flinched back and hugged my head closer. "Impertinent girl."

"Boy!" Zach snapped back.

"Unless she takes up my offer, yes." The crab scuttled back down the side of the bathtub. "I'll come back tonight for your answer." The tap of crab leg on porcelain faded away, as quickly as it'd come.

Zach let go of my head and stood up to peer down into the bathtub. I did too, my hooves sliding on the slick bathroom tile. The bathtub was empty again. The fairy had gone.

There was a knock on the door leading to the hall. "Zach, everything all right?" It was the female teacher, the one whose name I couldn't remember.

Zach turned to me and put a finger to his lips. "Wait here," he said in a whisper. He left and shut the bathroom door behind him. His voice came through the door, muffled, but still understandable. "Fine, Mrs. Derman."

The teacher responded, but I couldn't hear her. Then Zachary's voice came again, clearer. "Princess and I are going to stay here until her mom gets here. I'm going to withdraw from the competition."

Shouting for a bit, then murmurs. Then I heard the door shut, and the door to the bathroom opened again. "We'll stay here until your mom gets here. Hopefully she knows what to do."

She did not. Neither did any of the oracles, soothsayers, or other spiritual and magical advisors that my mom had made the acquaintance of over the years that she called for advice. The three of us huddled in that hotel room, the two of them tried to keep me calm until dark.

Finally the sun went down, and I transformed back to human. My mom hugged me, crying. "Take the service honey. You can't live like this."

"No, I already explained this to Zach. I can't risk losing you. Besides," I admitted, sitting on the bed between them and taking both her hands. "I actually quite like being a deer. You've never felt it. Bounding through the woods, nature all around you. No human worries weighing you down. It's amazing. I don't want to give that up."

So, I didn't. When the fairy came back, I told her where to shove it. And she couldn't do anything about it. It's in all the old tales if you know where to look. Fairy magic can't affect you if you don't make a deal with it. She scuttled about, turning herself into a giant crab and clacking her claws at us, yelling threats. But it was all bluff and bluster. Eventually, she got tired and left, and I went home with my mom and Zach.

My mom bought us a hundred acre property out in the California desert. During the day, I bound around my own private nature reserve with a pretty gold collar around my neck. A few times Zach put a leash on me and walked me around the downtown of the little town nearest our property. Word got around pretty fast that the pretty white doe was his pet and not to be messed with. At night I turn back to human, and get to spend the night with my adorable husband.

Zach still does shooting competition sometimes. I watch them on TV at home, wishing I could be there with him. It's the only time now I regret my curse. He's gotten pretty good. Made it to nationals a few times. Brought in enough money from sponsorships that we don't have to rely on my parents anymore.

I love my life now and wouldn't change anything. But still, fairies can kiss my white-tailed ass. And if I never see another one, it will be too soon.

Fate's answer

This story was originally published by me in
a Discord roleplay server in 2020.

The cards were spread out in a diamond in front of me,
their meaning clear and terrible. And yet, I couldn't
give this reading to the earnest young Eastern dragon
in front of me.

The only illumination came from a dim magical
lantern hanging above the table that put us in a
circle of light. Beyond, it seemed we hung in a dark
void, except for the dull bustle of dragons about their
business in the night market that hummed in the
background.

My friend Cyrano sat perched on the edge of
their stool, their short tail wagging behind them in
excitement as they tilted their head down to examine
the drawings on my cards. "Bastiaan," they said,
glancing up at me, their white face shockingly bright
against the gloom. "Your cards are so pretty."

"Sebastiaan, or Bast, please." I grinned at them,
showing off my overgrown fangs. Normally I didn't let

the customer's small talk distract me from the task at hand, but this time I was grateful for the distraction. "I commissioned the deck special from an artist friend of mine before I started out. I had hoped at the time that beautiful cards might offset my appearance and draw in more customers..."

They barked out a laugh. "But they don't see the cards till they're already in the tent and committed."

"Just so." I inclined my head. "But still, the cards make me happy." I gently touched the painted surface of one card that depicted a waterwheel tossing a spray of mist into a sunlit sky. Too cheerful of an image for the fate it represented just now.

"So, what does it mean?" They asked, gesturing at the table.

"This layout shows the past, present, and possible futures," I said, hovering a claw over each card in the middle row as I mentioned each in turn. "And the points of the diamond above and below are potential and reasons behind the question you asked." I frowned down at the cards and shook my head. "But this reading is flawed. I'm going to redo it." I swept the cards together and tucked them at random back into the deck even as my client protested.

"Hey, why not tell me what they mean first?" Cyrano cried out.

I shrugged and twitched my shoulder to throw back my mantle fur to keep it out of the way and began shuffling the deck. "I couldn't interpret it," I lied, still shuffling. When I felt it time I spread the entire deck out on the small table in one practiced sweep of my hand. "Pick five cards, keeping your question in mind as you do so."

Cyrano took their time doing as I asked, casting their hand across the line of cards multiple times before plucking out their chosen cards. I stacked the rest of the deck back together and set it aside, then took the cards from Cyrano and laid them out in the same diamond pattern, face down. Only once I felt each was in the proper place did I turn them over. My stomach sank as each card revealed itself as the same one as before. Even the waterwheel mocked me.

"Huh, that's odd." Cyrano's tail stopped wagging and curled around their stool.

I scowled down at the cards, then stood and pulled down the blanket that covered the entrance to my canopy when I was giving readings and snapped my fingers to turn off the magical lantern.

The lights from the night market's bobbing lanterns shown in and bisected the table almost perfectly. Almost like the fates were trying to make a point.

Cyrano disappeared into the shadows except for their bone white facial markings, making them look like a floating skull.

"No charge," I said, pointing my arm out at the market. "I'll try again for tomorrow when the fates are feeling less capricious, if you'd still like a reading."

"Bast," Cyrano said, their eyes wide. "What's wrong? You're scaring me."

I glanced out at the twilight sky, the stars already starting to disappear as the sky brightened to dawn. Around me my neighbors were already starting to pack up. Good. I was ready to go regardless.

I ran my fingers through my mantle, straightening it as Cyrano and I stared at each other. I sighed in defeat at the young one's defiant expression and sat back down on my stool, my shoulder's slumping.

"Your question, that you refused to tell me, I remind you. Your reading might be more accurate if you shared." I paused, but my young friend just shook their head. "Then your enterprise is in dire circumstances." I tapped the tower card, a horn being struck by lightning. "The future is in fates wheel," I moved my hand to the waterwheel card and its cheerful spray of water, "and nothing you can do now can change the outcome. Things are balanced on a knife's edge, the dark might take it all or it might blossom into a shining light. Only time will tell. The rest of the cards all speak to that fate."

Cyrano laughed and stood. "That doesn't sound so bad. Why so glum and mysterious about it?"

I sputtered, gathering up the cards. "I was unable to give an answer. Some fortune teller I am."

"Some things are destined to remain in darkness until the time is right. Like the dawn, the sun comes up when it will, not when you want it to." Cyrano clapped a hand on my back as they dropped coins on the table and left, humming happily, their tail wagging.

Cyrano's Companion

This story was originally published by me in a Discord roleplay server in 2020.

Cyrano flew down to the night market twisting with excitement. They had a big date coming up and wanted to get a tarot reading from their friend Bast beforehand. The wind ruffled his fur, streaming past their eyes as they dive-bombed down towards the colorful lights of the market, a splash of color and sound maring the darkness that still covered the rest of the town.

They shifted to anthro form right before he landed outside the gates of the market and then paused to straighten their coat. The market was crowded with dragons buying and selling, but Cyrano ignored them all, intent on threading their way through to Bast's tent.

The flap on the door was tied back, indicating Bast wasn't with another client so Cyrano ducked inside, but stopped dead at what they found there. Bast stood in the corner, his back to the tent entrance. In the corner was a new addition from the last time Cyrano had come: a massive bird perch now took up one corner of the room, and a purple vulture clung to one branch. The vulture's head was turned up, eyes closed, as Bast stroked the underside of its neck.

"Whose a pretty bird?" Bast cooed in a singsong. The bird squawked and fluffed out its wings.

"Get a girlfriend finally, Bast?" Cyrano joked, putting their hands on their hips.

Bast whirled, fur flying and tangling with some of the outstretched branches of the vulture's perch. His ears went back and he narrowed his eyes as Cyrano.

"Perhaps I did," he snorted as he began discreetly running his claws through his fur to tug it free of the wooden perches. The vulture made a little squawk again and hopped over to Bast's shoulder. Bast smiled at the thing and scratched the feathers on its chest lightly before looking back to Cyrano.

"I take it you're here for a reading then?" Bast said. The vulture hunched its shoulders and eyed Cyrano warily.

"I was," Cyrano said, staring at the bird, "but this is far more interesting. What possessed you to buy a vulture?"

"I didn't buy a vulture." Bast rolled his eyes and sat down at his table, the vulture still balanced on his shoulder, and began shuffling his cards.

"Bast, that is clearly a vulture." Cyrano sat down across from him, eyes fixed on the bird.

"Her name is Dulcet." Bast laid the deck in front of Cyrano. "Cut."

Only half paying attention to the cards, Cyrano cut the deck in three places and handed it back to

Bast. They knew he should have been focused on his question, but the bird demanded all their attention.

"If you didn't buy her, then where'd you get her?" Cyrano asked.

Bast began laying out the cards. "I didn't. I hatched her from a familiar egg."

"Really?" Cyrano propped their head on their fists and grinned. "And you got a vulture? That's adorable."

Bast started turning over cards and explaining what they meant, but Cyrano wasn't even listening, eyes fixed on the bird. Dulcet clearly loved Bast. She cooed and rubbed her head and neck against the side of Bast's head.

"That'll be five coins," Bast said, holding out a hand. Cyrano had brought just enough to pay for the reading, and dumped the coins out into Bast's outstretched hand without even counting them. They hadn't heard a word Bast had said, but who cared. A familiar! A cute creature to hang out with. Cyrano wanted one now, desperately.

"Where'd you get the egg?" Cyrano pressed, standing with their hands resting on the table, leaning closer to the vulture and Bast.

"If you must know, I..." Bast paused for a moment. "I found it. I thought it was a rock at first, but..." he grinned and scritched Dulcet again, "Lucullan down the way set me straight."

"Lucky." Cyrano muttered, slumping back down to their seat and crossing their arms. "I want a cute pet, too."

Bast sighed. "There's a vendor in the market selling them for five coins, if you want to get your own. And you'll also need to buy a gift for it, to coax it into hatching."

Cyrano pouted and turned their empty wallet over to stare down into it. "I seem to be a bit short." They looked up at Bast with their best pathetic expression. Eyes wide, mouth slightly turned down, ears half cocked. "Could I borrow ten coins? I seem to be a bit short."

Bast gave them an exasperated look, raising his eyebrows and shaking his head. "You really only brought five coins to the market?"

"Only planned to get a reading." Cyrano shrugged and gave Bast a wolfish grin, showing their fangs. Bast's fangs were much more impressive, and Cyrano had always been a little jealous. "Please?" They batted their eyes at Bast. "I'll pay you back next time I come."

Bast sighed and shook his head. "Fine, here." He dropped Cyrano's five coins onto the table then bent to retrieve his cashbox and fished out five more. "After you get the egg and food, take it to the graveyard and you'll hatch a vulture."

"The graveyard?" Cyrano recoiled, wrinkling his snout. "Ugh, do I have to?"

"The egg responds to the environment and the gift you give it. That's how I got my vulture. If you go somewhere else, you'll get a different familiar."

"With my luck I'd get a rat skeleton or something if I go to the graveyard."

Bast laughed. "Fine, whatever. Maybe ask the egg vendor where to go then." With that he shooed Cyrano out of his tent after giving them a quickly sketched map with directions to the egg vendor.

Cyrano eventually found her on the edge of the market and purchased their own egg-rock. If Bast hadn't mentioned that he'd thought it was a rock at first, Cyrano would have thought the vendor was trying to scam him. Yet, despite looking like a rock, when held the egg was warm and Cyrano swore he could feel a faint-yet-steady heartbeat coming from the little rock.

Next, the gift. The egg vendor sold a selection of things as well. Cyrano scoffed at the food and tools. No, they wanted a smart animal. A companion more than a pet was what he really wanted, so he got a book to give the familiar as a gift.

"What now?" Cyrano asked, staring down at the book and egg clutched in either hand.

"Now, take it somewhere to hatch it. The location you take it influences what hatches from the egg," the vendor said.

"Can you tell me what animal I'll get?"

The vendor shook her head, bells in her horns jingling. "Sorry. It's up to the egg itself what you'll get from it."

"I need an interesting location then..." Cyrano muttered, changing and flying away. "I want a creature that will impress everyone I come across."

So many places in the world. Cyrano flew about for a bit, enjoying the heat from the sun. The portal to the mortal realm was interesting. They'd been there once and the swirling blue colors certainly made for quite the show. Still, they hesitated.

Then it hit them. What was more impressive than a volcano! Cyrano twisted in the sky and shot north.

They landed on the lip of the crater and craned their head to stare down at the lava bubbling far beneath him. Perfect. They set down the egg, placed the book of knowledge next to it, and waited.

Several long hours later, a bright blue tortoise hatched from the egg. Cyrano was enchanted and delighted. So much better than a stupid vulture.

The Fish and the Candles

This story was originally published by me in a Discord roleplay server in 2020.

Once upon a time, there was a mighty and powerful Eastern dragon Lord that ruled over the delta. Her son grew into a powerful dragon, with great crown horns and glowing runes twisting around his entire form. Now old enough to find a mate, the Lord told her son that she would gift him her most precious possession once he had found the one he would be soulbonded to.

The Lord's son searched the land for many years before meeting a special dragon that he fell in love with. She was of common birth, the daughter of a pair of farmers living in the delta, and had no magic of her own, and only plain brown fur and common horns.

When the Son brought her home, announcing his intention to soulbond with her, the Lord denied them permission.

The Son and his love had prepared their offerings for the elder, scented candles that they'd made together from the fruits of the lover's parent's farm. The Lord stole the candles and flew away, following the twisting delta rivers until they reached the sea. She tossed the candles into the ocean waves before flying back home.

Returning back home where the Son was trying to comfort his love about the loss of their hard work, the Lord announced that only if the gods returned the candles would she bless their soulbond.

However, a faithful servant of the Son had seen the Lord stealing the candles and had followed her at a distance. That night, the servant told the Son and the lover where the Lord had dumped the offering. The Son and his lover that very night flew out to the sea with nets, where they desperately cast about, trying to dredge up the candles, but all they caught was a giant sea bass, longer than a full-grown dragon.

Dejected, they returned back to the Lord's house with the fish, thinking to at least cook it up as a feast to feed the Lord in an effort to win her approval. However, when they cut the fish open, the offering candles, every last one of them, tumbled out.

The Son and his lover hid the candles and cooked the fish, then once it had cooled, hid the candles again inside its belly. That morning they presented the meal to the Lord for breakfast. When she cut into it with her claws, the scent of the candles filled the room. The Lord saw the candles inside the fish and conceded that their union was indeed blessed by the Gods.

The Lord presented her own Grand House to the happy couple as a present. There, after the eldest dragon had blessed their mating ritual and the couple had soulbonded, the couple hatched and raised a dozen happy babies.

Origin of the Lights

This story was originally published in the 2021 Furvana conbook. Furvana is the name of the con's mascot.

Furvana sat around a bonfire with a group of their friends. They were on the beach at night, tired from a long day of swimming, splashing, and playing in the ocean that lay just a few feet away. Now they all relaxed, enjoying each other's company while watching the stars twinkling overhead. The surf lapped quietly nearby, a soothing lullaby. Furvana lay sprawled against the legs of their best friend, who sat in a chair behind them idly rubbing the top of their head and their ears with both paws. Their friend's tail snaked around from the hole in the back of the chair so that the tip, with little wings, rested in Furvana's lap. Furvana hugged the fluffy mass to their chest.

Someone was telling a ghost story about a group of friends that had stumbled across the haunted cabin in the woods, and each time their friend got scared and jumped, the wings on his tail flapped and tickled

Furvana's muzzle. The silliness took the scary bite out of the storyteller's story, but Furvana didn't mind. They didn't really like being scared, but did like the excuse to hug their friend, or their friend's tail is this case.

Then something amazing began to happen in the sky. It started at a point far in the distance, barely seen on the horizon. Shimmering lines of color, in red, green, blue, purple and more dripped across the sky in a slow, undulating waltz, expanding out from that small point until the entire northern half of the sky was a riot of colors that overlay the twinkling stars behind.

The storyteller trailed off, her story forgotten, as the lights flashed and twirled overhead.

"What are those?" Furvana chuffed almost inaudibly. The lights reminded them of something that they used to know, long ago. They hadn't lived here long, so they were still occasionally caught off guard by new things.

"No idea," their friend yipped back, startling Furvana who put their ears back. They'd been so fascinated with the lights that they'd forgotten anyone else was even around. "I've never seen anything like them before.

The rippling lights reflected off the rolling waves, creating an almost perfect circle of color between sea and sky, the two halves slightly out of sync as the waves distorted the lines.

"What's that?" the storyteller asked, and Furvana turned their attention back to the sky. The lights seemed to be twisting, forming shapes in the night sky. At first it was just a circle, but it compressed and morphed until—

"It's us!" Furvana's friend gasped. Furvana had to agree, the outline, with its big, cone-shaped ears, the outline of tiny wings coming off their feet and thick tail, did very much resemble their own outlines.

"No," the storyteller said, her voice dropping with awe, "It has to be two dragons battling far overhead. Or gods dueling for control of the night sky."

"Psah," another said, standing and moving to stand between the group and the lights. She struck a pose, balancing on one foot, her tail arched behind her, and slowly began extending her other leg while outstretching her arms upwards. "If it's gods they're dancing, not battling." With that she kicked off into a graceful pirouette, spraying sand behind her. Her form was silhouetted in black against the colors. The shape of the lights mirrored her outline in celestial glory high overhead as she danced away down the beach, spinning and kicking in time to a beat that only she could hear, chasing the light's reflections on the surf.

"Ghosts!" Furvana's friend cried, leaning over to hug Furvana's head and look down at them. The white of his eyes stood out in the firelight against his darker blue face fur. "Like in the storyteller's story. Except they're haunting the sky. The lines lead back to the afterworld."

The storyteller nodded thoughtfully. "Perhaps that is why the shapes look like foxes, like us."

"It's a portent of good things to come!" a fourth said.

"No, it's light from the stars cooking their dinner," a fifth said, and his stomach growled audibly. His ears went back and his tail curled around his feet, and he sat back down.

Furvana listened to all of these explanations, but none of them seemed right to them. They looked up at the lights, spinning out across the sky like a... "Web!" they said out loud without meaning to.

Everyone stopped what they were doing and turned to look at Furvana. Even their friend leaned further forward so they could peer down at Furvana. "Did you remember something, Furvana?"

"No, I don't know where that came from," they said.

"So, we've all made a guess," Furvana's friend said, his tail twitching in Furvana's lap. "Except you. What do you think they are?"

"Maybe you're all partially right," Furvana mused, letting their mind drift, pretending they were surfing the lights like waves. "Can't it be all of those things at once?"

"How's that?" their friend asked, rubbing between Furvana's ears again and making sure to hit their favorite spot. Furvana chirped happily, the dancing lights reflecting off their eyes as they craned their head back to catch the whole show in all its glory. Then all of a sudden a story hit them.

"There was once a god that wanted to be a water fox," Furvana said. The story seemed to be spun from the lights, and Furvana just the translator. "She spun herself in a cocoon to transform herself. The cocoon flew through the sky, burning as it fell, and when it landed, the god was a fox. But she left pieces of herself in the sky, a ghost of the god part of herself that now lives in the sky, watching over the world as its protector, to keep her new mortal form safe. The lights are her waving hello, telling us that she'll always be over us in spirit."

"That's a lovely story." The storyteller sounded awed. "Do you mind if I use it, to tell next time we see the lights?" Overhead the light show was dying down, only a few streaks of green remained, and then they were gone and once again only the twinkling of the stars against the black of the sky remained.

Furvana smiled and hugged their friend's tail. "I'd be honored."

Also By Ian Madison Keller

Flower's Fang Series

Book 1:
F
lower's Fang

Book 2: Flower's Curse

Arara's Prequel Story: Snow Flower

Dragonsbane Saga

Book 1:

The Dragon Tax

Book 2: Dragons Ahoy

Book 3: Dragon Fried Cheese

Book 4:

S
ilence of the Dragon

Riastel Prequel Story: Red Dragon
Sybil Prequel Story: Black Dragon

Other Works

Shark Week: 13 Ocean Themed Furry Short Stories

The Fluffpocalypse and Other Stories: 7 Furry Horror Short Stories

Sam Digger: Beaver Detective

Furry Fiction is Everywhere: A Step-by-Step Guide to Writing Anthropomorphic Characters
Origin of the Lights and Other Stories: 12 Furry Short Stories

About the Author

IAN MADISON KELLER is a long-time furry author. He has published over a dozen novels since 2015, and has had over fifteen short stories published in various furry publications like ROAR, Zooscape, and CLAW. Ian is a trans man and loves to write trans and queer characters in his stories.

He lives in the Pacific Northwest with his husband and a pack of vicious Chihuahua mixes. When not writing he can be found sewing plushies, at the dog park, or bicycling around the woods.

Learn more at http://MadisonKeller.net

Sign up for Ian's newsletter at http://madisonkeller.-net/newsletter/